VOICES
FROM THE
LOST
HORIZON

VOICES
FROM THE
LOST
HORIZON

STORIES AND SONGS OF THE
GREAT ANDAMANESE

ANVITA ABBI

Illustrations by SUBIR ROY

NIYOGI
BOOKS

Published by

NIYOGI BOOKS

Block D, Building No. 77
Okhla Industrial Area, Phase-I
New Delhi-110 020, INDIA
Tel: 91-11-26816301, 26818960
Email: niyogibooks@gmail.com
Website: www.niyogibooksindia.com

Text & Photographs © Anvita Abbi

Editor: Arunima Ghosh
Design: Nabanita Das
Cover & illustrations: Subir Roy

ISBN: 978-93-91125-06-6
Publication: 2021

Printed at: Niyogi Offset Pvt. Ltd., New Delhi, India

'Don't let the language slip away, keep a hold on it'
Boa Sr, the last speaker of Bo from the
Great Andamanese language family

***

To Ahir,
My grandson on his sixteenth birthday
Who has grown up listening to my Andaman escapades

Contents

Foreword	9
Preface	13
Introduction	19
The Great Narrative of Phertajido	40
The Tale of Juro, the Head Hunter	54
The Tale of Maya Lephai	61
Maya Jiro Mithe	68
Dik and Kaunmo	78
Golat and Tae Daniel	82
Maya Boro and Jurwachom	86
Dik, the Demon, and the Fish	93
The Water God Maya-Kobo and Jire	98
When We hunted Dugong: A real story	103
Echoes of the Past	109
Endnotes	145
Appendix: The Original and Line-to-Line English Translation	147
A1 The Great Narrative of Phertajido	147
A2 The Tale of Maya Lephai	155
A3 Maya Jiro Mithe	161
A4 The Water God Maya-Kobo and Jire	167
A5 When We Hunted Dugong	169
Afterword	172
Acknowledgements	175

Foreword

Fifteen years ago, Boa Sr, the last speaker of Bo, a language of the Great Andamanese family, made an impassioned appeal to her interlocutor: 'Don't let the language slip away, keep a hold on it.' Elder Boa Sr passed away on 26 January 2010. As far as we know, there are no other living speakers or even 'rememberers' of the Bo language.

This tragic reality is offset—albeit only modestly—by the fact that Boa Sr could not have made her petition to a listener better positioned to recognize and accept the challenge. For some years already, Boa Sr had been in conversation with internationally-celebrated linguist and award-winning champion of marginalized and Indigenous languages, Anvita Abbi. Since her first trip to the Andaman Islands in December 2001, Professor Abbi has worked tirelessly to ensure that the unique linguistic and cultural traditions of the Andamans would not vanish from human consciousness without record. *Voices from the Lost Horizon: Stories and Songs of the Great Andamanese*, taken together with Professor Abbi's large oeuvre of important and interdisciplinary publications, offers a tangible demonstration of this commitment.

This book brings together 10 rare stories and 46 songs in Great Andamanese, the only collection of its kind. Transmitting these precious teachings in ways that are appropriate, respectful, and ethical is both a privilege and an enormous responsibility. What does it mean to publish stories and songs in a language which has no more living speakers? To whom do these stories belong, and what conditions attach to their circulation and dissemination? And who are the intended readers? Professor Abbi does not shy away from engaging with such questions. She honours the memory and cultural knowledge of Nao Junior—who narrated all but one of the stories—and Boa Sr, the narrator of 'Dik the Demon', by inviting the reader into the complicated context of each recording session. Each telling is prefaced with a careful description of the circumstances of its sharing, however imperfect, conflicted and interrupted these may have been.

Reading these carefully composed translations of these Great Andamanese stories and songs, I was reminded of Wade Davis, my colleague at the University of British Columbia, who lyrically describes each language as 'an old growth forest of the mind, a watershed of thought, an entire ecosystem of spiritual possibilities.' In ways that are neither nostalgic nor bullish, Abbi shows these Great Andamanese stories and songs for what they are now, at this point in history, a partial remembering of a time when humans and the more-than-human world were in an intimate relation, implicated in each other's destinies.

The recorded elicitation sessions that Abbi shares with her readers speak to the humility of both the recorder and the recorded, forging human connections across vastly different cultures, languages and lived experiences. It is a testament to the patient compassion of the community knowledge holders and the sincerity of the visiting scholars that meaningful relationships took root despite the structural and hierarchical impediments that history has placed in their way. Abbi invites us to consider Nao Jr as a 'symbol of a priceless Indian heritage.' Her point is delicate, and indeed political. Throughout their lives, Nao Jr, Boa Sr and their relatives have been subjected to multiples waves of indignities, starting with the epidemics brought to the Andaman and Nicobar Islands by the British that devastated the local population; followed by the Japanese occupation of their homeland during World War II; and culminating in the forced relocation of their entire community to Strait Island, a small tribal reserve, by the Government of India, whose approach to the 'tribal' could be described as controversial to say the least. Abbi's work invites us to think through the implications and responsibilities of colonization and occupation—external and internal. If the Indian republic considered the late Nao Jr to have been its subject and citizen, then he must also be entitled to the benefits that accord to such membership. To my mind, there is no doubt that Nao Jr and Boa Sr deserve recognition as having made profound contributions to the complex and rich heritage of India.

While each story or song in this collection carries extraordinary beauty, the 'Great Narrative of Phertajido' has resonant quality unlike any other. A short but complex narrative of ethnogenesis, the story is suffused with emotion and themes of survival. We are introduced to Phertajido, the first man of the Andaman Islands, who originated from the hollow of a bamboo stalk. Given the violent depredations to which the

Indigenous communities of the Andaman Islands have been subjected over centuries—colonial, political, epidemiological, evangelical, and most recently, in the form of the 2004 tsunami, climatic—the bamboo motif seems particularly apt. As anthropologist and historian Alan Macfarlane has written, bamboo is a unique natural product and offers us a powerful metaphor to think with. At once incredibly strong, resilient, hardy and robust, bamboo is at the same time flexible, agile and malleable. No matter how much bamboo is warped by the wind, it always returns to its upright position, retaining its integrity. This same metaphor may be extended to the collaborative research undertaken by Nao Jr, Boa Sr and Anvita Abbi; while their creative partnership has required great adaptability and compromise as conditions around them have changed, its core structure—founded on truth and dignity—has remained unchanged. Thanks to this long-term and participatory research collaboration, a global readership knows something of the lives that Nao Jr and Boa Sr have lived.

Few Indigenous peoples have been as fortunate in their allocation of a resident linguist and advocate as the last speakers of Great Andamanese. For two decades now, Abbi has marshalled the full intellectual and strategic weight of her training, disciplinary expertise and socio-cultural capital to document, preserve and share with the world the voices, songs, stories and laughter of the Great Andamanese. We, the readers of *Voices from the Lost Horizon: Stories and Songs of the Great Andamanese*, are the beneficiaries.

Mark Turin
University of British Columbia, Vancouver

Preface

This is a collection of folk tales and songs of the Great Andamanese, a moribund language of the only surviving pre-Neolithic tribe, the remnants of the first migration out of Africa 70,000 years ago. When I visited the island in 2005, the surviving eight speakers informed us that due to loss of fluency in the language, the narrative power in any of the two languages that they used was already lost. None of the speakers was proficient enough to tell any tales, either in Great Andamanese or in Andamanese Hindi—the former was already on the brink of extinction, while the latter was a pidgin with broken linguistic structures. It was the most daunting and challenging task to extract stories from a tribe that had not heard any stories in the last 40–50 years. Hence, these stories and songs represent the first-ever collection rendered to the compiler by the Great Andamanese people in local settings. The compilation comes with audio and video recordings of the stories and songs to retain the originality and orality of the narratives.

With the extinction of storytellers and singers, as mentioned in the foreword, this is the only collection of 10 rare stories and 46 rare songs obtained in the native language. I was fortunate enough to elicit these stories in their lifetime when I visited them in Port Blair or the jungles of Strait Island. Each story is unique in its own way, as the oral narratives are different from those written or told in the mainstream languages.

The Great Andamanese people were hunters and gatherers till the mid-19th century. Their stories in the current manuscript represent the world of forest-dwellers as well as that of the seafarers. The evolution of the Great Andamanese has been very different from the agrarian and pastoral societies, which is well reflected in the tales.

All but one of the stories were narrated by Nao Junior, a male member of the society. Other members of the Great Andamanese community were neither willing to share folk tales, nor found any utility in remembering them. In such a challenging situation, it was a daunting task to elicit stories, comprehend the meanings and nuances of words and expressions, as well as appreciate a worldview far removed from ours. But without Nao Jr, we would have left the island without any folk tale. He was the only one who remembered the language and the names of various natural objects, including the names of the birds and fishes. He was a soft-spoken and very sensitive person, who eventually realized the importance of language documentation and helped us throughout our stay in the island despite the initial resistance. He could give us two creation tales—rather rare renderings. He eventually became quite enthusiastic in narrating the folk tales, so much so that he took a keen interest in the whole process of documentation so that I could record each of them very carefully and accurately. I have tried my best to capture the journey of elicitation and recording in the first chapter to familiarize the readers with the environment—the context in which the elicitation was made, as well as the frame of mind of the narrator.

Out of the 10 stories, only four were rendered in the bilingual mode viz. the Great Andamanese language and Andamanese Hindi. The rest were narrated to us in Andamanese Hindi only, as the narrator found himself incompetent to tell the whole story in his native language. As the elicitation progressed, the narrator gradually became more confident in his rendering. These stories are given in the book in simple transcription, followed by a line-by-line English translation. Hence, some stories are long, which have been provided with original renderings along with their English translations, while others are short, as only the English translation has been given here and the original Andamanese Hindi version (a kind of pidgin) has been held back. Some words have been retained in original for their resonance or their untranslatability. The songs have also been given in Roman transcription. Free English translation accompanies the original narratives and songs. Thus, the readers can read the stories in the original language or sing the songs in the Great Andamanese language. The book comes with interactive QR codes through which some of the audio-visual recordings can be accessed. These stories and songs will introduce the speakers to one of the oldest languages of the world.

The original renderings were transcribed in IPA (International Phonetic Alphabet) with interlinear translation followed by Devanagari, the script that is used for the written form of the language. However, to ensure user-friendliness, we have used Roman transcription for the Great Andamanese speech. These recordings of the songs and stories were done in the original environment. Because it is perhaps one of the oldest and the very first surviving languages of the people who inhabited Southeast Asia, its oral rendering is invaluable for any literary documentation.

These stories encode the worldview of the Great Andamanese society as they encapsulate history, philosophy, culture, beliefs, values, and power of judgment. Alas, the loss of language and its speakers with the ability to narrate has wiped out all these from the face of this earth permanently. By publishing these stories, we will be able to give life to some of the lost oral heritage of the vanishing world of the Great Andamanese.

This is the first time that Great Andamanese songs have been transcribed in Roman and translated in English, bringing to light a unique heritage. Most of the songs are from Boa Sr, the last speaker of the Bo language, who remembered some songs. There are two songs on turtle-hunting from a male, a Karen speaker, who is currently in his late 80s. He learned the Great Andamanese language in 1940 from one of the Great Andamanese elders and still remembered it when I met him in 2008. Unfortunately, the remaining members of the community neither speak the language, nor remember any tale or song.

The two key persons, Nao Jr and Boa Sr, who contributed to this volume, are no more in this world. I remember it vividly that while I was preparing the dictionary of the Great Andamanese language, I was informed that Nao Jr, who was in his 50s, succumbed to kidney failure and passed away on 22 January 2009. He was a symbol of a priceless Indian heritage and, in death, he carried away with him the knowledge and memories of an entire race. The world lost a precious gem from an ancient civilization. Later, on 26 January 2010, Boa Sr, aged 83, also passed away due to a prolonged illness. It is sad that both these speakers left for the heavenly abode much before their time. The only solace that I have today is that we travelled together in reviving the memories of an ancient civilization.

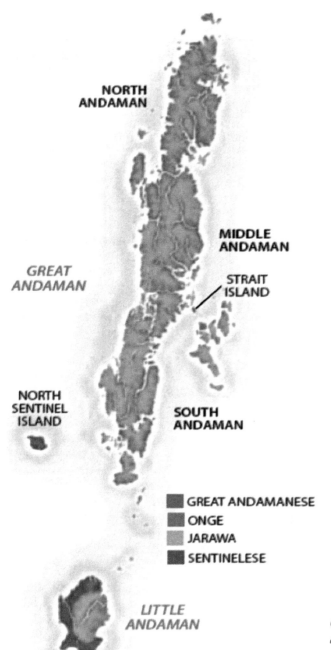

NORTH
ANDAMAN

MIDDLE
ANDAMAN

GREAT
ANDAMAN

STRAIT
ISLAND

NORTH
SENTINEL
ISLAND

SOUTH
ANDAMAN

GREAT ANDAMANESE
ONGE
JARAWA
SENTINELESE

LITTLE
ANDAMAN

*Geographical
distribution of
Andaman Islanders in
the present times*

Introduction

Connecting with the Oldest Civilization of the World

THE ANDAMAN AND NICOBAR ISLANDS

A cluster of approximately 324 islands and islets in the Bay of Bengal, running from north to south and located southeast of the Indian subcontinent, constitutes the Andaman and Nicobar Islands. The Andaman Islands lie between 10°13'–13°30N latitude and 90°15'–93°10E longitude. These are truly oceanic islands, never having been connected to the mainland during Pleistocene glaciations. They are separated from the Malay Peninsula by the Andaman Sea, an arm of the Bay of Bengal, and are part of the union territory of the Andaman and Nicobar Islands which belong to India. The Andaman Islands are broadly divisible into two sets of groups, Great Andaman and Little Andaman.

The area covered by the Andaman Islands is made up of island clusters. From north to south, the various islands are North Andaman, Middle Andaman, South Andaman, Baratang, Ritchie Archipelago, and North and South Sentinel. Collectively, these are called the Great Andaman. The close proximity of these islands to each other creates the impression of one island, a fact that unfortunately motivated the government to build the Andaman Grand Trunk Road, which robbed the tribes of their basic resources due to rampant deforestation. The road resulted in shifting the Jarawa to the western coast of the Island, losing in this process the accessibility of the jungles towards the east.

The capital city of the Andaman Islands is Port Blair, located in the south of the islands at a distance of 1255 km from Kolkata. Approximately 65 km south from the city of Port Blair in the Great Andaman is the island of Little Andaman, which is home to the Onges, one of the four tribes of the Andaman Islands.

ABOUT THE GREAT ANDAMANESE

The Andaman Islands—the Great Andaman, Little Andaman, and North Sentinel Islands have been home for millenniums to four tribes viz. the Great Andamanese, Onge, Jarawa, and Sentinelese. Their languages are known by the same name as that of the names of the tribes. Both Jarawa and Onge call themselves Ang, and hence, I refer to their languages as Angan languages. Their languages are genealogically related to each other, but distinct from the Great Andamanese languages. Sentinelese have protected themselves from outside intervention so far and thus, our knowledge about them is very minimal. All four tribes belong to the Negrito ethnic race.

The Great Andamanese, according to the population geneticists, are the remnants of the first migration from Africa that took place 70,000 years ago (Thangaraja et al. 2005). They are the very first settlers of Southeast Asia and have lived in the islands in isolation practically with no contact with the outside world till the late 19th century when the

British made Great Andaman the penal colony, commonly known as Kala Pani, in 1858. The language of the Great Andamanese people is called the Great Andamanese, the same name as the tribe.

Thus, Great Andamanese is a generic term representing 10 languages among a family of languages that were once spoken by 10 different tribes living in the north, south, and middle of the Great Andaman Islands. These languages were mutually intelligible like a link in a chain. Thus, the two ends of the chain were distant from each other, but the links in between were close to each other in a mutual intelligibility scale.

Present-day Great Andamanese (PGA) is a mixture of four northern varieties of the Great Andamanese languages, i.e., Jeru, Khora, Bo, and Sare. Alas, we recently lost the last speaker of Khora, the late Boro Sr, the last speaker of the Bo language, the late Boa Sr, and the last speaker of Sare, the late Licho. Most of the central and the southern varieties were lost in the mid-30s. As the speakers of the North Andaman were dislocated from their ancestral places and were relocated in the 70s in one small island named Strait Island, communication was established by the mixed-language, incorporating features of all four. Because the language is a mixed one, the term Present-day Great Andamanese (PGA) was used to refer to this language, which had drawn its lexicon from Khora, Bo, Jeru, and Sare languages, the four North Andamanese varieties of the Great Andamanese language family, but the grammar was based on Jeru. Refer to Fig. 1 on 'Great Andamanese Language Family' given in the next page. Number in the brackets show the year of the extinction of that language.

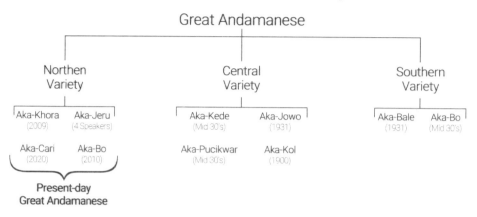

Fig. 1 Present-day Great Andamanese and its regional varieties

PGA displays rare grammatical features (for details refer to Abbi 2013). Perhaps most importantly, PGA is a unique language; there is strong linguistic and genetic evidence to suggest that the people of the Andaman Islands represent a distinct genetic group who populated the Andaman Islands tens of thousands of years ago.

The PGA language, commonly known as Jeru, Jero, or Andamanese, is currently spoken in the city of Port Blair and Strait Island, which is 53 nautical miles away from Port Blair. There were eight speakers of the language in a community of 53 members in Great Andaman when we started our work in 2005.[1] There were some semi-speakers who could understand the language, but could not speak it fluently.

Unlike Jarawa and Onge, Great Andamanese is a moribund language and breathing its last breath. The Great Andamanese people were hunters and gatherers till the end of the 19th century, a period just before the intensive contact with the British, when the latter established the penal colony in Port Blair in 1858. At present, except

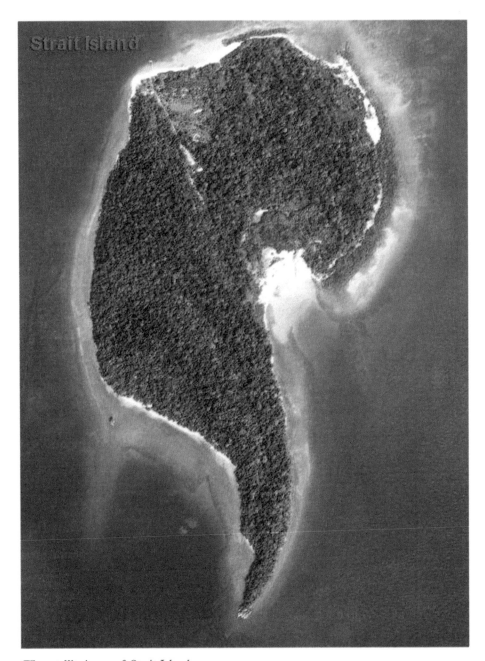

The satellite image of Strait Island

the Jarawas and the Sentinelese, no Andamanese tribe can be called hunter and gatherer in the true sense. On any given day, two Great Andamanese males still prefer to hunt in the sea and the forest, but not for their livelihood. The community is heavily dependent on the subsidy provided by the government for their daily needs.

The present generation of the Great Andamanese speakers is the result of intermarriages among these North Andamanese tribes. The Government of India encouraged this practice to save the dwindling population and settled the entire population of the Great Andamanese in Strait Island in the mid-70s. There is a thread of strong mutual intelligibility running through the speakers. However, complete comprehensibility across speakers is missing. As the language is in a moribund state, that is, inter-generational transfer no longer exists and adults do not get any opportunity to speak it. A low level of competence and the lack of motivation are additional factors that discourage speakers from using their heritage language. At most, the Great Andamanese tribe symbolizes the language with its past history. Unfortunately, the language is considered something to relish and identify with, like an icon, but not something to be used in daily life. However, it was observed that adult speakers above the age of 45 use it as a code language in front of outsiders. In this kind of a scenario, it was a challenging task to elicit data, record sounds, confirm and reconfirm the elicited data, and to extract songs and stories.

When language is almost lost to its community, the memory of stories evaporates first. One is tempted to ask the question: when a language is on the verge of extinction, what dies along with the language—is it the history, culture, ecological base, knowledge of the biodiversity, ethnolinguistic practices, or the identity of the community, or all of these? Most definitely and unfortunately, it is all of these features that get extinguished along with the extinction of the language. Cultural beliefs, values, knowledge, and behaviour concerning the environment are expressed in language. As the transmission of a language to the younger generation ceases, its loss leads to the loss of beliefs, values, and knowledge.

Linguists maintain that there is an inextricable relationship between language and environment. Although this is more easily recognized in the indigenous, minority, or local communities that maintain close ties with their natural environment, this complex web of connections is prevalent throughout the globe. Currently, the culture associated with the traditional language is under threat due to the shift in the power dynamics in language, which can lead to the death of the heritage language itself. The death of a language signifies the closure of the link it had with its ancient heritage and knowledge-base.

MY LIFE WITH THE ANDAMANESE

The fieldwork in the Andamans was not easy. The first trip that we made to the Andaman Islands was in December 2001, under the project 'Linguistic Survey of the Tribal and Contact Languages of the Andaman Islands' (2001–2002) to conduct a pilot survey of the languages spoken in Great Andaman and Little Andaman.[2] I was assisted by two of my students. On our way to Little Andaman, where the Onges live, we traversed through the forests of the island, saw water snakes more

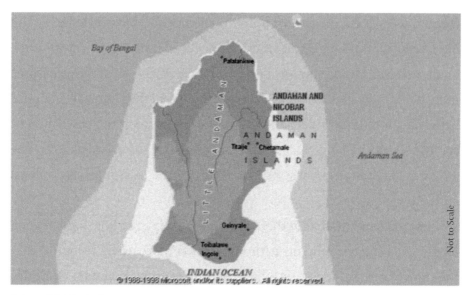

Map of Little Andaman

poisonous than any cobra, crossed narrow creeks laden with crocodiles, and lived in shanties regularly visited by snakes, scorpions, and leeches. In our ignorance, we had armed ourselves only against mosquitoes by taking along coils and mosquito repellents. Who knew that the simple act of dipping one's feet in the water to cool oneself would invite water snakes? Apparently, the sea water under the jetty at the Dugong Creek was full of poisonous water snakes. Thanks to the local who saved my life by pulling me off the jetty at the right time!

When we travelled to Little Andaman, 100 miles away from the city of Port Blair, we had to use every mode of transport to reach the place. First, there was a night journey by ship, followed by a bus ride for a few kilometres, and then a boat ride in narrow creeks with thick mangroves along the coastline. The water in the creeks was clear enough to see

Eliciting data and stories from an Onge boy at Dugong Creek, Little Andaman (January 2002)

several crocodiles resting at the creek-bed. We were, obviously, very frightened by the sight. At some distance, we also spotted one crocodile basking leisurely in the sun. The worst was a 7-mile walk on the western side of the seashore of the Little Andaman, necessitated by the possibility that the boat might capsize in the rough sea. It was an arduous task to walk on the sand with our luggage on our heads. Luckily, our ration of food supplies was carried by one of the helpers provided by the administration. We were instructed to climb mangrove trees, in case the water swelled up and covered the walking area on the shore. None of us knew how to climb trees. When we were returning from Little Andaman, there was a high tide and the water started submerging the shore, gradually swallowing up our path inch by inch. None of us were adept at swimming in the sea either, and we had to run for our lives.

Mangroves roots are extremely unruly and entangle one's feet, so one cannot even walk on them. We were battling for life, and many times, I wondered how many of my friends and colleagues back in Delhi could have endured an experience like this. But we did it and that is the most important achievement.

Life at Little Andaman was not easy in many other ways as well. The guest house that we were given to live in was in a dilapidated state, with windows without wire mesh, with an unlit kitchen without any infrastructure, and no place to take bath. The ration that we took along did not last for more than four days, albeit the ingenuity of the cook who came with us to help. Our initial attempt was to stock everything including the supply of rice and onions for 8–9 days. When the cook reported to me that we would have to leave for Port Blair by the next ship as the supply was finished, least did he know that he was dealing with a stubborn linguist, who would not succumb to such threats. We turned into hunters and gatherers ourselves and realized how difficult it was to look for food in the jungle every day. After two days of eating jackfruits and papayas, we took recourse to catch fish, which were aplenty in that island. Some of the best and most beautiful looking fish—to the point of not wanting to kill them—made our meals for the rest of the days we spent working in Little Andaman. Thanks to the Onges, who lent us their fishing net.

However, it was in Strait Island, my *karma bhoomi*, the core area of my fieldwork, where I learned most about the Great Andamanese people, their culture, their beliefs, and their language. Before I describe the tales of collecting tales, let me describe who the Great Andamanese people are and how significant they had been in forming the history of human migration and human civilization.

OUR LIFE ON STRAIT ISLAND

During the first trip in 2001, I learnt that the languages of the islands, especially Great Andamanese, were endangered; but above all, I realized that the clock was ticking very fast and I should document the language before it was completely lost. Soon I applied for a grant from the School of Oriental and African Studies, London (SOAS), under their Endangered Language Documentation Programme (ELDP). I was fortunate enough to get the grant for the project *Vanishing Voices of the Great Andamanese* (VOGA), and we set out to work in December 2004[3]. Alas, the tsunami hit the Andamans on 26 December 2004 and our visit was postponed till March 2005. The fieldwork to elicit language data was undertaken between the period of 2005 and 2009. The aim was to prepare a multilingual dictionary, write an extensive ethnolinguistic grammar, document the language in audio and video formats, document indigenous knowledge about the forest, sea, and life pattern and, if possible, to elicit folk songs and stories.

We were discouraged by friends and relatives from going to Andaman and Nicobar soon after the tsunami. The entire nation was going through a fear psychosis, but our determination was strong and unshakeable. We found out that all the members of the Great Andamanese tribe were transferred from Strait Island to Port Blair and were located under one roof in the post-tsunami relief camp at Adi Basera. This information boosted our morale, as we could ascertain the

Great Andamanese community at Strait Island (Photograph by Alok Das)

availability of all the speakers residing in one place. Given the context, we collected several words relating to the tsunami, words used to identify the trees which proved to be life saviours on the fateful day, and scores of words for seascape and sea-related matters. We also took the opportunity to converse with almost all the old members of the present Great Andamanese tribe as they were living under one roof. Boa Sr and others obliged us by narrating how they saved themselves on the fateful morning of 26 December 2004 when the tsunami arrived. These narrations proved helpful in obtaining new words for the dictionary[4].

The team members[5] spent varying amounts of time on the island during these four years, but I spent the longest as, after the initial phase of fieldwork, due to the adverse living conditions in the islands, lack of social activities, and boredom, it became difficult for my research assistants to sustain their interest in the work. I could never stay longer than three months at a time, because of the constraints that Jawaharlal Nehru University has on its faculty.[6] Thus, I made several trips to the Andaman Islands and worked in shifts. This helped me to verify data at intervals and gave me the possibility of spending time in the jungle in different seasons, which, I realized later, facilitated me to obtain names of seasonal flowers, birds, and fish. The entire process of collation, sifting, slicing of sounds, and digitization of the elicited material was carried out at the Jawaharlal Nehru University, New Delhi.

The speakers of the language were sceptical about our venture in the initial stages of our fieldwork, but became cooperative and friendly subsequently. As we motivated them to go down the memory lane and converse about topics such as hunting, naming a child, and boat-building, which they had forgotten, a stage was reached when they realized that their language was in the process of being revived. This became evident when our key narrator admitted that by telling us a few stories, he could remember the language which he had thought he had forgotten.

As part of the project on *Vanishing Voices of the Great Andamanese* (2005–2009), we were to spend some time on Strait Island, which is 53 nautical miles from the city of Port Blair and to which public visits are banned. To reach the island one has to take a ship, which sails only twice a week. The ship does not have Strait Island as its ultimate destination, but only stops over there briefly en route to the two North Andaman Island ports viz. Mayabandar and Diglipur. It was in December 2005 and again in January 2006 that I went to Strait Island along with three of my team members—Alok Das, Narayan Chaudhury, and Abhishek Avatans. The Andaman Adim Janjati Vikas Samiti (AAJVS), the tribal welfare society, had arranged for accommodation for us in a government guesthouse. The situation of this guest house was deplorable. There were two bare-walled rooms, each with a dirty, but functional, attached bathroom, windows without screens, and a hard, wooden bed to sleep on. The only other furniture in the room were four plastic chairs for each of us. Birds, bats, and insects could freely wander into our rooms at night, since we could not even imagine closing the windows, given the sultry, humid weather and the absence of fans. The good old Indian mosquito net was the only shield we had against these intruders. The mere luxuries here were the cotton sheets that we were given to cover ourselves and two-hour electric supply generated by solar power, which we could use from 9 pm every night to charge our recorders, cameras, and other equipment. We had to travel to Strait Island fully equipped with food supplies, such as daal, spices, cooking oil, rice, tea, sugar, milk powder, soap, and kerosene to light the stove. The team members shared the job of cooking and cleaning the utensils. It is here that I learnt how to light the pump stove.

On my first visit to the island, I was disappointed to see that most of the adults spoke in Andamanese Hindi. When I asked why they did not speak in their indigenous language, they admitted that they had forgotten it all. On pressing a little hard, I realized that they remembered the words, but perhaps not full sentences. I said, 'Ok, you can teach me words,' and thus started my journey of learning Great Andamanese.

Our life at Strait Island guesthouse; serving meal to Abhishek (January 2006)

Narayan eliciting the first version of Phertajido in Strait Island guesthouse (January 2006)

It also turned out to be a journey of language revival, as some elders started speaking among themselves to use it as a code language so that I don't understand their communication. This was encouraging, as I came to know they still had competency in the language, but their situation did not allow them to practice it. I grabbed the opportunity and gradually convinced them to translate a few Hindi sentences in Great Andamanese.

Many words were collected during our trips to the jungle, where we asked the speakers to identify a plant, bush, or tree, and speak about its uses in daily life. Similarly, we spent long hours by the seashore to help them remember the words used to identify several kinds of crabs, fish, reptiles, and sea creatures. In the evenings, I would accompany my tribal friends on fishing expeditions on the north side of Strait Island. As I visited the island at different times of the year, I was exposed to different varieties of fish each time. The Great Andamanese became so accustomed to my recording the names of fish and snapping pictures of the catch that if I happened not to be on the seashore, they would come to my room with their catch before cooking it and ask me to take a picture. By this time, documenting the language had become a joint project of the Great Andamanese tribe and mine. Joint outings into the jungles and marshes introduced me to several creepers, plants, and their uses, and crabs, snails, and worms. I am happy to see that all that, which was collected then, forms a significant piece of information now in the trilingual talking dictionary that I prepared[7].

The variety and abundance of sea life found in the islands is both a source of sustenance to the tribes as well as a hazard. I would like to mention two endangered mammals that the Andamanese are very fond of hunting—the Andamanese pygmy hog (*Sus andamaenensis*) and a sea mammal known as *dugong* or sea cow. Reptile life is rather rich as many species of snakes, monitor lizards, large turtles, and saltwater crocodiles inhabit these islands. Birds of the sea variety and jungle variety are a familiar sight. Much later, I was inspired to collect the names of many endemic birds, because one of the folk tales informed me that birds were considered to be the ancestors of the Great Andamanese. Not only I collected the names of many birds, which are documented in a beautifully produced book, but also various attributes of the birds, their feeding and nesting habits, characteristics of flora and seashores. A variety of fish, crabs, toads, and frogs abound in the Andaman Sea that serves as food to many. Names of all these creatures appear in the dictionary that we prepared. According to a few experts, Andamanese flora and fauna present a somewhat impoverished version of its counterpart in the Burmese Arakan region to the north. This is an important clue: in the geological past and especially during the Pleistocene epoch, the Andamans must have been a peninsula connected to the Burmese mainland or at least an island separated from the mainland by only a narrow passage.

ABOUT THE SPEAKERS

The present-day Great Andamanese tribes have an interesting mixed heritage, which has resulted in their varying degree of language competence. Not all nine members, whom we met in Strait Island, were fluent speakers of Jeru or PGA, as they did not come from the same clan speaking the same variety. Initially, they all called themselves 'Jero' or 'Jeru' speakers, because some government official had instructed them to report this when asked about their mother tongue by an outsider. My pilot survey revealed very clearly that the community had speakers from primarily four distinct tribes—Jero, Khora, Bo, and Sare—all dislocated from their lands in North Andaman by the Government of India in the mid-1970s. Thus, the speakers did not hail from the same

One of the trips to the eastern part of Strait Island after the tsunami (2007)

linguistic group. Intermarriages among the members had created the ideal situation of language being mixed and of bilingual mixtures. We soon realized that a Jero speaker may have descended from a Jero father and a Bo mother, or a Khora speaker may have descended from a Khora father and a Bo mother, then married a Sare man. Each speaker had a distinct genealogical history and each had a different language as the first language. All the contributing languages have produced a mutually intelligible version of a lingua franca known as Great Andamanese. In this scenario, fieldwork was a daunting task. Our oldest speaker, Boa Sr, had not conversed with anyone in her ancestral Bo language for the last 30–40 years and longed for someone to talk to. Many of the words that she used were not comprehensible to the others. She once confessed to me that if she got hold of a person who could speak her language, she would talk to him or her the whole day and the whole night without a break. She was at times very lonely, but kept smiling. I vividly remember that Boa Sr could never complete a sentence without a hearty laugh. Her full-throated laughter echoes in my ears even today.

Because the current language is an admixture of three or four North Andamanese languages, I have used 'Great Andamanese' as an umbrella term, not empowering any one particular language to dominate as a reference marker. The members of the tribe are not only exposed to Andamanese Hindi, but also feel comfortable conversing in it. Andamanese Hindi, far removed from the standard variety of Hindi, is the lingua franca of all the Andaman and Nicobar islanders. In this complex linguistic scenario, it was very difficult to elicit narration, stories, words, phrases, and sentences, and then understand the nuances to get close to the worldview of the hunter and gatherer society. Fortunately, we could succeed in our mission, because of the faith that the speakers had in our job and their love for their language, which was revived after my frequent visits to them.

My urge and insistence to communicate in Great Andamanese brought back many memories and incidences to them, some of them are locked in this book. I remember I encountered this sentence, 'We have spoken in our language more with you than we ever spoke before' many times. Currently, the Great Andamanese people communicate mainly in Andamanese Hindi.

MY TRYST WITH THE DYING LANGUAGE

I have lived in the jungles of Strait Island with almost none of the facilities of modern life, far from any communication network and without any of the basic necessities. The sense of isolation and dejection at times was discouraging, but the friendship that I developed with the tribes was a ray of hope that sustained me through the hardships. I can never thank them enough for exposing their world to me.

There was, unfortunately, only one prime narrator, Nao Jr, who could remember any folk tales. The oldest member of the tribe, Boa Sr remembered songs, but not any folk tale; however, later she corroborated one folk tale, which was rendered to us by Nao Jr. Perhaps, Nao Jr could have remembered more tales, but his untimely death due to liver failure snatched the most fluent speaker of the language from all of us. I have tried my best to inform the readers about the process of elicitation in a dying language and how I shared the journey of storytelling by a reluctant narrator to a die-hard one. Towards the end of this journey, it appeared that the treasure trove of stories in the memory of Nao Jr opened up, as he wanted to tell more and more, but the vagaries of life pulled me back to Delhi, and soon after, I lost him forever.

The greatest challenge that I faced was translating incidents of ancient foregone days as encapsulated here in the narration, 'When we hunted Dugong: A real story' and its appendix (A5). Translating other folk stories was not easy either as the context, myths, and beliefs of the tribes were distanced from us physically, emotionally, and philosophically. I had to see the world from the eyes of Nao Jr and, at times, I found myself incompetent in doing so. To preserve the memories of Nao Jr and Boa Sr, and their contribution to the revival of this endangered language, a song, in audio-visual medium, has been presented at the end of each story (Chapter 2 onwards) in a QR code to be scanned, to share the invaluable experience of knowing the last speakers of Great Andamanese.

I hope the readers will enjoy sharing this ancient world of cognition and appreciate that although most of it is already lost to the world, it is fortunately locked in the grammar[8], dictionary[9], the book on names and classification of the Andamanese birds[10], and now in this book of ancient tales and songs.

The Great Narrative of Phertajido

A Creation Myth

*T*his was the month of January in 2006. I, with my team members, had gone to Strait Island, where some Great Andamanese people were staying distributed in eight households. There were more children than adults and it seemed no one had any work to do, as food supply was given to the community as a subsidy. The men used to spend time either fishing at the jetty or roaming in the jungle, which was neither very dense nor very large. Women sat under a tree, gossiping, and children either played cricket with a make-belief bat or just surrounded the chatting women. The whole atmosphere was very relaxed and time seemed to pass very slowly. Despite the small adult population, the ones who were in Strait were those who had some competency in their heritage language that kindled hope of finding some folk tales. I had found out that out of all the adult folks, only Nao Jr claimed to remember one story. Only one! Well, I decided something is better than nothing. Thus, I approached his hut with expectations and hope.

Nao Jr was seemingly always busy, either 'on duty' in the only medical unit that Strait Island had, distributing medicines in case there was a need for anyone on the island, or fishing in the early morning or late

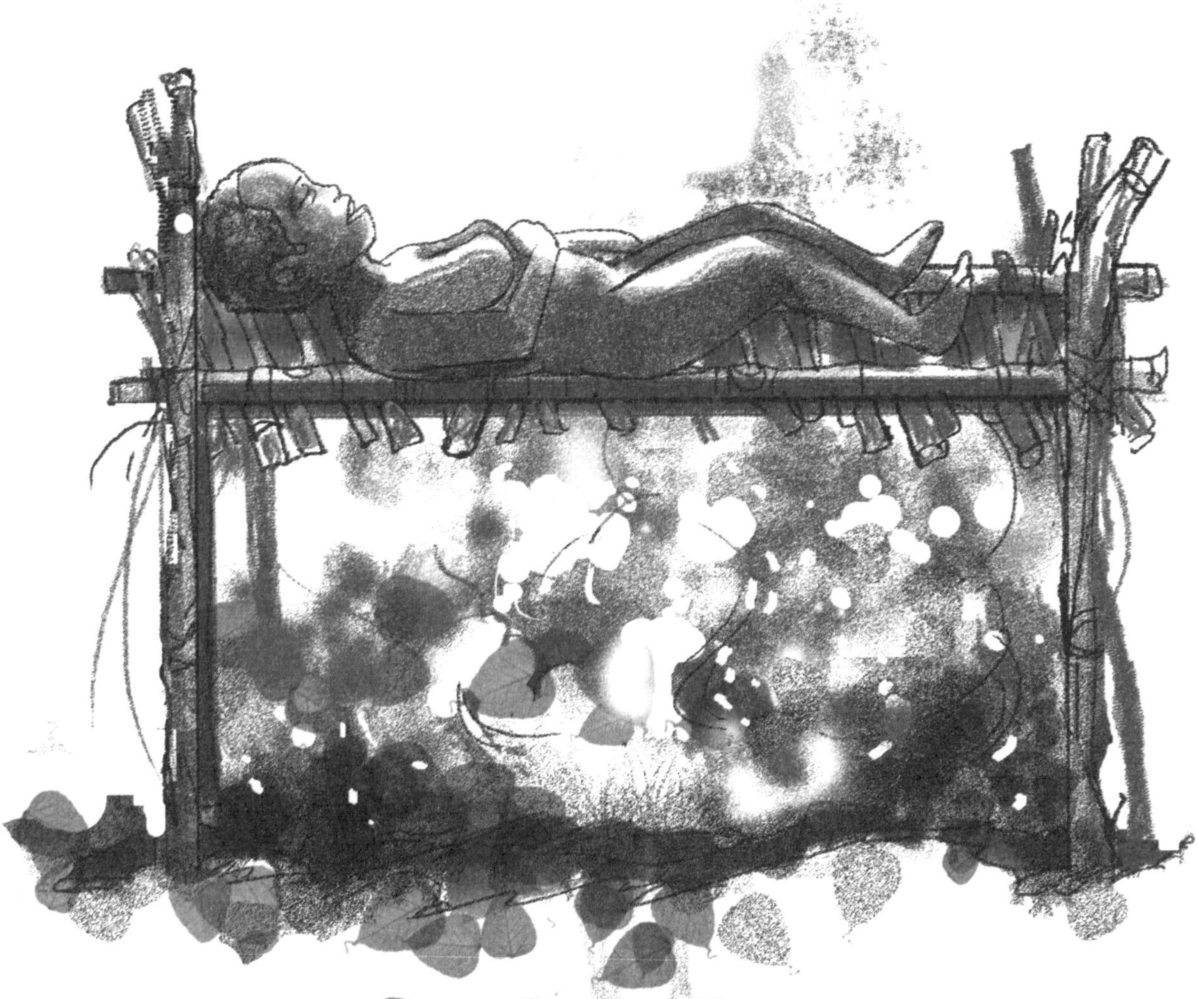

evening, or just sleeping, which was his favourite pass-time. He agreed to help me record the folk tale only after 9 at night and I agreed to his terms, as I was excited to find at least one person in the entire habitat of eight households who claimed to remember a tale. He promised to visit me in the guesthouse. I was very anxious to receive him at the stipulated time.

I remember distinctly that it was 21 January 2006. Nao came to the guesthouse, thinking that he would finish the job in one evening. Little did he know that linguists have the bad habit of checking each and every word and phrase that is uttered. In the first sitting, he tried to narrate the story in Andamanese Hindi. He would halt in between, groping for the right words or phrases. When he was not satisfied with the Hindi version, he would suddenly revert to the appropriate Andamanese word. This was rather exciting and educational for me. The long-lost language was getting revived gradually in an ancient tale. I never expected this!

The loud choruses of the crickets and frogs had begun in the tsunami-created marshes and swamps behind our guesthouse; the power had been switched off and we were all sitting in the dark. We knew it was past 11 pm. We used to get electricity only for two hours. Nao wanted to retire. I extracted a promise from him to visit us the next day, at his convenience, but with the Andamanese version and not the Hindi one. He said he had forgotten it all. When I insisted that he could attempt to remember it at night while going to bed, he agreed to try but was sure that his memory would fail him. 'Chaaliis saal se sunaa nahiin, kaun bolega? (It has been 40 years since I have heard it; who can narrate it?)' He was sure he would disappoint me.

Then came the next day. I was making some grammar notes sitting on the wooden bed in the afternoon. I saw Nao standing at my door with an expectant look on his face. The moment I looked up, he said in Hindi, 'Kuch kuch yaad aataa hai (I can remember a little).' I invited him in and then we sat around the bed, turning it into a makeshift table. He started narrating the same story in short Great Andamanese phrases, not very fluently, but mixed with Hindi. Narayan, my student, assisted me in recording and transcribing the story. This is how our long journey of the Great Andamanese narration started, a journey into the past. I would interrupt him to get Hindi equivalents and he could, with a 90 percent success rate, render them. It took us several days, to get the full version of the narration of 'Phertajido' and the subsequent word-for-word translation. Sometimes, we would have our sessions in the afternoon and sometimes after 9 pm, as he was always busy fishing by the Strait Island jetty after sunset. This was a great story and I could see he loved narrating it.[11]

The translated version of this story had some gaps, which I realized only after coming back to Delhi. I decided to go through the entire process again during the next trip. I was lucky enough as Nao obliged me during my next trip to Port Blair in December 2006, almost 11 months after our previous visit.

On reaching Port Blair in December 2006, I discovered that Nao was in Strait Island and not in Port Blair as I was informed by a tribal friend on the phone before I left Delhi. The AAJVS officials not only failed to honour my already sanctioned permit to visit Strait Island but were also on the lookout to catch and arrest me if I pursued

Nao Jr with the author in Strait Island (January 2006)

my research. No one in the mainland would believe that a researcher could be arrested for hearing a story from the Great Andamanese tribes for work. Under the pretext of safeguarding the protected tribes, the concerned official would disregard the sanction given to us by the Home Ministry and would expect us to grease his palms. I neither had the means nor the inclinations to oblige him.[12]

There was no way of informing Nao of my arrival in Port Blair. Unfortunately, Strait Island had no phone connections. The only wireless communication that the island had, was in the hands of the government officials. I had no option but to visit the Port Blair jetty and take a chance and see if I could run into any of my tribal friends on the

Reya (on my left) and Renge (on my right), the two daughters of the queen of the tribe (Adi Basera, Port Blair, December 2005)

ship. Ships for Strait Island leave very early in the morning at about 5:45 am. It was 19 December 2006; I reached the jetty much before the stipulated time. A crew member from one of the ships recognized me. By then, many local officials, especially those who worked on ships and boats, had started recognizing me as a friend of the Great Andamanese tribes. As soon as this man, a ticket checker at the departure gate saw me, he indicated towards the next ship moored in the distance and said,

'Go and see Reya. She is going to Strait Island.' This was a girl from the Great Andamanese tribe, whom I knew very well and who had married a Bengali man. I ran towards her, lest I lose her. She immediately recognized me and greeted me with a namaste. She introduced me to her husband. She asked me in Hindi, 'Kab aayaa (when did you come)?' Reya is one of those Great Andamanese tribal girls, who loves to amalgamate herself into our society and is happy to forget her heritage language. I told her that I desperately wanted to see Nili (the pet name of Nao). She informed me that Nao was on Strait Island and had no plans of visiting Port Blair. My world was falling to pieces.

I knew requesting the administration to transport Nao Jr to Port Blair would not help. I knew that getting permission to travel to Strait Island will be equally difficult, as some officers-in-charge were against any research on these tribes. It is a shame that the members of these tribes are kept as captives in their own land and are restricted from meeting other Indian citizens. Had it not been for the initiative of the Great Andamanese themselves, they would have never befriended locals and visitors like us. I immediately fished out a piece of paper from my purse, wrote a note in Hindi in bold letters, and gave it to Reya to pass it on to Nao. I told her to ask him to have it read out to him by one of the school-going children. I also told her that the sole purpose of my trip to the Andamans was to meet Nao and my other tribal friends, but Nao in particular. She promised to deliver the message.

It was not until 21 December 2006 that I got an opportunity to meet Nao Jr, who did respond to my request and made the journey to Port Blair just for me. He came to the Circuit House, where I was staying and told me that he had received my letter. He needed some money desperately and I obliged. He looked frail and sad. When I commented on his health, he immediately complained of loneliness and desolateness. I took him to my room, and we talked of days gone by, his solitary life on Strait Island and the irritating officers. He was missing my student Abhishek, and had tears in his eyes when he mentioned his name. He told me the Phertajido story all over again and helped me to translate it word to word. This story was very dear to him, I think; it satisfied his internal desire of creating a soulmate for himself. I remember vividly that when I stood up to bid him goodbye that evening, he wiped his eyes with the back of his hand. When I saw this, I asked him point-blank, 'You love this story, don't you?' He nodded in affirmation. He found that creating one's partner according to one's liking was the best part of the story. When I commented, 'Perhaps you like this story so much because you also feel that you could create a partner of your choice and not one like Boa, right?'[13], he said in Hindi, 'This is the greatest love story I have ever come across in my life.' His voice, choked with emotion, was hardly audible.

Nao visited me for the next two days to complete this story. When he visited the Circuit House on the 23rd, in the evening, he was very drunk and was in no state to help me with my translation. He was very sorry for himself and promised to visit me the next day. He did come the next day with his son, Bea, aged 8, who used to go to the Vivekanand School at Port Blair. We finished inter-linearizing the story, while Bea watched us, and I further collected some words for birds and reptiles for my dictionary. Bea helped me with some words, and I realized that he knew a couple of names of the birds, because

Nao had been teaching him whenever they visited the jungle on Strait Island. Following is the running English translation of the story. A conscious effort has been made to keep it close to the original as much as possible.

THE GREAT NARRATIVE OF PHERTAJIDO

In ancient times, there lived a man named Phertajido[14]. He was the first man of the Andaman Islands. He originated from the hollow of a bamboo. He roamed here and there, searched for food, and lived alone. He spent his time making bows and arrows.

One day, he shot the arrows here and there in all directions. The next day, he went to search for the shot arrows. As he looked for them, he found a spring and drank water from it, and thus, discovered drinking water.

He went to look for more of the arrows and found one hidden in the roots of a potato plant. He thus found the potato and took some with him.

He looked for more of the shot arrows. This time, he found the third arrow in a heap of incense (*dhoop*). He took a bit of the *dhoop* with him.

He went to look for more of the shot arrows. He found a very fine soil of *kaut*. He took some of this also with him. He made pots out of the soil. He dried them to harden. When the pots dried and became hard, he put the potatoes in the pot. He lit the fire with the help of the *dhoop* that he had collected. He then put water in the pot and boiled the potatoes. He ate those potatoes and thus enjoyed the meal of boiled potatoes.

While eating potatoes, an idea came to him—to carve a sculpture from the remaining fine soil of *kaut*.

He wasted no time and, in a few days, made a human look-alike dummy out of the *kaut* soil.

He put this dummy on a raised platform and burnt some fire under it, to dry it well. Thereafter, he resumed his bow-making.

He would look at the dummy on the platform again and again, while he continued making his bows and arrows. He ensured that the dummy was lying on the platform and did not fall down. He would occasionally get up and go to the platform to put some more wood into the fire, and then, would come back to his bow-shaving job. After a while, as he looked back again, he was taken by surprise. The platform shook as the female figure of *kaut* turned over her side. Phertajido was overwhelmed. He was immensely satisfied with his work. He stood up again to kindle the fire and complete the job of drying the figure.

When he got tired of making bows, he went into the jungle to hunt, leaving the *kaut* figurine on the platform, for it to be dried completely. He found a game and proceeded home with it.

As he approached home, he glanced from a distance at the platform. It was empty. He was shocked. He felt dejected and lost.

He put down the game and sighed, 'Where did Kaut disappear?' With a heavy heart, he sat down on the ground. He did not know what to do next. He was oblivious of the fact that the lady, Kaut, was inside the house.

Kaut saw Phertajido from inside the house and started laughing. She laughed and laughed until she got tired of it. Surprised,

Phertajido looked back. He saw Kaut sitting inside the house laughing merrily.

Phertajido ran to her. He embraced Kaut and burst into tears, out of the sheer joy of discovering her. After that, both of them started living together as husband and wife. They had many children. Their children married among themselves and, thus, their clan increased by leaps and bounds.

Phertajido once asked his wife, Kaut, to make ropes.

He went to bring a creeper, *pharako*, found in the jungle, which is good for making rope, and came back with it.

He asked his wife to peel the creeper and prepare a rope for it.

His wife followed his advice and made a very long rope. It was so long that it coiled into a heap.

Phertajido tied a stone at the head of the rope. He swirled and swirled the rope several times and finally threw it up in the sky. He pulled back the rope and found that it was entangled somewhere and would not come down. He twisted the rope to make it harder. The rope tightened and stiffened. He tugged at it, but the rope would not move. He knew that the rope was stuck somewhere.

He went to call Kaut. He said to her, 'I will go up, above the clouds to see the place above us. I will find out how it looks like. I will go there tomorrow.'

The next day, he climbed up above the clouds with the help of the *pharako* rope.

He saw the place and was surprised to find many people like himself.

He came back to the earth and told his wife about this. He told her that the place above them was nice and there were many people, like the people of Andaman. He suggested to her that both of them should go there.

Kaut did not like his suggestion. She said, 'How can we leave our children's place?'

Phertajido said, 'We will convince our children and then we will go.'

He gathered his children in one place and said, 'My dear children, please keep silent for a while. Your father and your mother are speaking to you. We will no longer stay here on this earth. We will go up above the clouds. You should live your life well here. Our time here is done. Now it is time for us to go.'

Thus saying, they went up above the clouds by climbing the rope. Once they reached the top, they cut it off from above.

***

Note: This creation myth was the very first story that Nao Jr narrated to me in broken sentences, but somehow, he completed its first version on the night of 21 January 2006. Nao was so fascinated by this particular narrative, that he never tired of telling it, as he thought this was one of the greatest love stories that he had ever heard in his life. He told me that creating one's partner according to one's own wishes was the best part of the story. He had tears in his eyes, when he narrated this tale. The story was collected in many sessions by me and Narayan Chaudhary. In many respects, it is a complete story, as it mentions the five basic elements of life, that is, fire, water, earth, space, and air. The climax of the

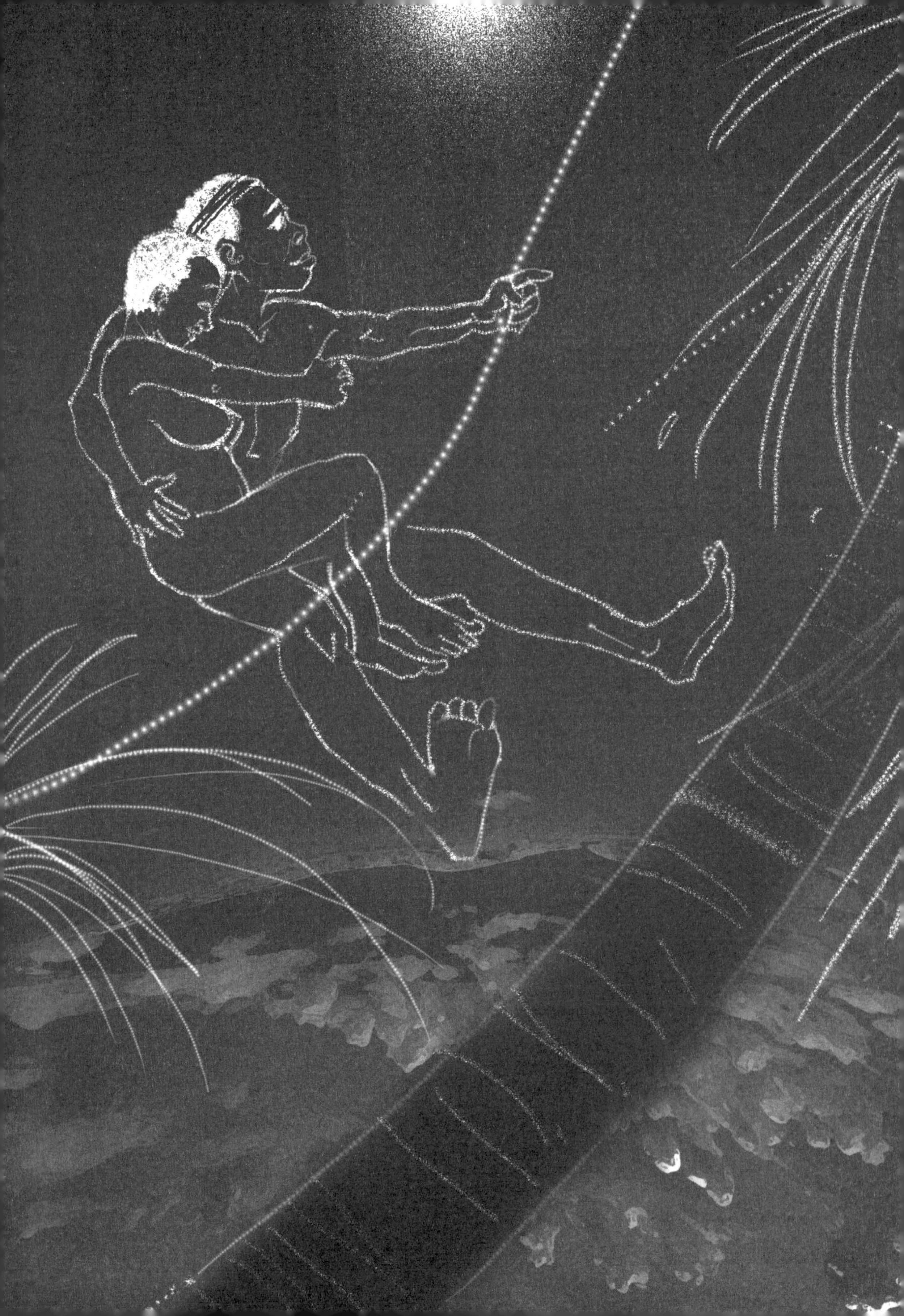

story is very philosophical. After spending a very fruitful and satisfying life, the protagonist decides to leave this world for another, without any possibility of coming back.

The original version of the story in Great Andamanese language with line-by-line translation in English is available in A1 of the Appendix.

Song 1: *a ḍure kaiyo laṛuka, ḍure kaiyo laṛuka, ḍure kaiyo laṛuka*
Meaning: This place is not good for living.
Singer: Boa Sr
Tribe: Bo

Scan the QR code
for the audio-visual
recording of this song

The Tale of Juro, the Headhunter

Narrated by Nao Jr on 25-12-06

O n the Christmas afternoon of 2006, Nao visited me again, accompanied by his son and, to my surprise, volunteered to narrate a new story of Juro, the headhunter. I shelved my linguistic work and sat down with my notebook. He instructed me, to my amusement, to switch on the recorder. He wanted in return a gift of a mobile phone. I promised to present him one and I kept my promise. The story of Juro was a bonanza for me, as I had never expected to hear anything after the story of Phertajido. This is one of the stories, where cannibalism was very evident. While narrating the story, he tried to establish the similarity between Juro and the Hindu goddess, Kali, for my understanding, when I asked how a woman could eat human flesh. I did not like the comparison as I told him that Kali never ate human flesh. He did not believe me, but I did not want to land up in an argument, as I wanted to focus on the elicitation of the story of Juro. He was not sure whether Juro wore the necklace of human skulls as Goddess Kali did. This story also reveals the superstition *that people, who die unexpectedly, are born again, or turn into ghosts to trouble the community. To avoid this, it is enjoined that the dead must be cremated and not buried. This ensures the complete annihilation of the person concerned. From the story, I learned that there were four kinds of funerals in their society.*

1. *When a person dies of a natural death or in illness, s/he is buried in the earth ('boa-phong' meaning 'hole in the earth').*

2. *When a person dies while hunting/killing, then s/he is put on a platform made on a tree ('machaan' in Hindi) and burnt.*

3. *When a person dies because of choking on a fishbone, their body is taken to a particular place near Mayabandar in the northern part of the Andaman Islands and left for a month on a tree for vultures to eat. The bones are collected after a month.*

4. *When children pass away, they are not buried initially; they are left untouched for a few days, then they are cremated.*

Juro's story raised mixed feelings of remorse and pity. Juro's son loved his mother, but could not bear her atrocious habits of headhunting and, thus, he became instrumental in her killing. Nao thought what he did was right and beneficial for the society. I was amazed at the way he compared Juro with the Hindu goddess, Kali, repeatedly. Although I found little similarity between the two, I didn't contradict him.

THE TALE OF JURO, THE HEADHUNTER

There was a woman called Juro, who lived in the forest. She was a headhunter. She would go to the seashore and catch young women and men to satisfy her appetite. While she was pregnant with a baby, she killed her husband and ate him up.

She eventually delivered a baby boy, whom she loved immensely. She continued to hunt humans from the seashore. She had four arms. One of the arms had a large *siro-bun* or seashell; another one had a *keo* or dagger; the third one adorned a lech or bow, and the fourth one was free to hold arrows.

As the child grew up, he noticed Juro regularly visiting the seashore and bringing back meat in good quantity. Once he asked his mother what meat she had been serving him. She replied that it was boar's meat. The boy was not convinced as the meat looked very different from that of boar. He also noticed that she often brought back human skulls in her hands. Once he secretly followed his mother to the seashore and saw her hunting humans.

He got really scared, as by now, he was married and had a child. He was scared that one day Juro might eat her grandchild. He was also scared for the community, as he realized that one day, no one would

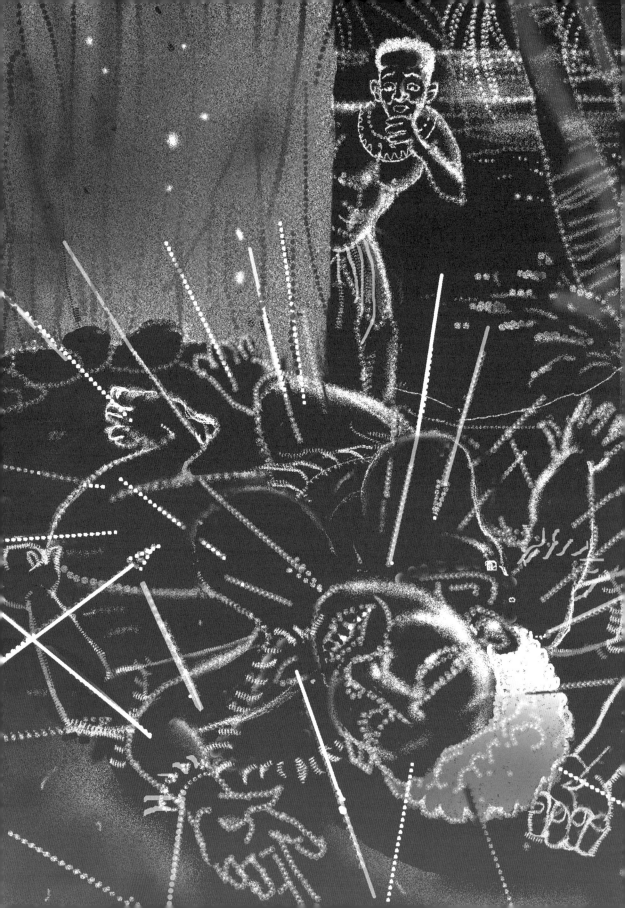

be left alive and the community may vanish totally. The place would be bereft of humans.

One fine day, he went to the village by the seashore and met the people of the village. He came to know that the village folk were very worried, because they were losing young men and women every day. No one could solve the mystery of the young population disappearing. Seeing their misery, he confided in them and told them about Juro's heinous behaviour.

The villagers believed him and asked him to suggest a remedy. He suggested that on an afternoon when his mother would be fast asleep, he would hide her weapons: the *siro-bun*, the *keo*, and the lech. She would be powerless without these arms. The villagers could then kill her and salvage the community from future destruction. The village folk liked his idea and decided to put the plan into action to get rid of Juro on a particular day.

Finally, the day for Juro's killing arrived. On that day, the boy was very sad, as he knew that he was going to lose his mother for good. Juro noticed his melancholic mood and asked him what the matter was. He just shook his head and replied, 'Nothing.'

He then went deep into the forest and hid himself. As promised, he took along all the weapons used by his mother and hid them in the forest.

The villagers came at the stipulated time and pierced Juro's body with innumerable arrows. There were so many arrows that one could not see her body properly.

Juro's son returned from the jungle and saw his mother's body gored by arrows. He had tears in his eyes, but he knew that he had to sacrifice his mother for the benefit of the human community.

He asked the villagers not to bury her in the earth lest she is reborn to rise again. He knew that Juro had special powers, of resurrection. Hence, he suggested to them that she should be burnt. The villagers put Juro's body on a raised platform (*machaan*). Her son insisted that all the weapons used by his mother should be also cremated along with her body.

The villagers followed his advice and then lit up the pyre. Juro's body was thus burnt to ashes. It was ironic that Juro was destroyed by the help of her son, who loved his mother immensely.

As time flew by, Juro's son became the father of many children. Both his family and the villagers lived fearlessly thereafter.

Song 2: *iyaya khiṭong kora cheraiyaya, khiṭong kora cheraiyaya, khiṭong kora cheraiyaya*
Meaning: Ya, Ya! (I) Have been working with bamboo stalks. I am tired and my hands are burning.
Singer: Boa Sr
Tribe: Bo
Boa Sr hailed from Mayabandar which is known for bamboo groves. She is sharing her experience of working in the grove when she was in Mayabunder (north Andaman). She is complaining of being very tired, while her hands hurt with a burning sensation.

Scan the QR code for the audio-visual recording of this song

The Tale of Maya Lephai

Narrated by Nao Jr on 29 January 2007

*N*ao completed this story in five days from 29 January 2007 to 02 February 2007. Every time Nao would leave for home, I would remind him to think of his parents before sleeping, how they hunted together in the sea and how his mother or grandmother must have narrated stories to him as a little child. My zeal for getting more and more infected him. One early morning, I had not even had my morning

Recording the story of Maya Lephai (Port Blair Circuit House HUDDO 2006)

cup of tea when he knocked on my door. His eyes were red and he looked disturbed. When I opened the door, he said, 'Madam, I could not sleep the whole night as I remembered this story and you have to listen to me.' What more could I have asked for?

I invited him in and made him comfortable by offering him a cup of tea. Over tea, he told me that he was trying to remember the story of 'Maya Lephai', which was narrated to him by his Abba (the father) when he was about seven years old. He told me that he liked the story very much even then, but had somehow forgotten all about it. His bloodshot eyes told me how he must have waited for dawn to break to come and narrate the tale of Maya Lephai to me. He first narrated it in Andamanese Hindi, so that I could understand it easily. He then gave it to me phrase by phrase in Great Andamanese, followed by the Hindi translation. I was amazed at the organized way in which he gave the information. He was better than many of us in the educated world. Whenever I got stuck, he would repeat and explain. The story has many dialogues and Nao obliged me by delivering each one of them with the proper intonation. Furthermore, he would put the earphones in his ears and ask me to rewind the recording, so that he could listen to his voice. Sometimes, he used to hear his rendering to remember the next episode or sequence in the story. All this was very educational for me. He had learnt to use the digital audio recorder and was assisting me unknowingly to achieve the near-perfect version.

When he was describing the final scene, he was lost in his world. I could see he was in a trance as if we had all vanished from the room, and he was transported to the hills of Bontaing (an indigenous name of the north side of the Jarawa Reserve in the Middle Andamans, near Bluff Island).

THE TALE OF MAYA LEPHAI

Lephai was a young man who loved a girl immensely. He wanted to marry her though his friends warned him that the girl was seen with another man and did not bear a good reputation. He did not believe his friends and said, 'No, no, I am going to marry her,' and he did so eventually. They had four children thereafter, two boys and two girls.

One fine day, he went hunting in the jungle to catch some game for his children. Somehow, he got delayed in coming home. When he came back, he found his wife missing. When he looked inside the house, he found his children crying and there was no sign of their mother. He asked them,

'Why are you crying?'

The children replied, 'Our mother has left.'

He inquired, 'Where did she go?'

The children replied, 'We don't know.'

Hearing this, Lephai said, 'Try to be quiet and have patience. I am sure she must have gone to her parents. I will go and look for her.'

Actually, his wife had run away with a man called Noe.

Lephai looked for his wife everywhere, but could not trace her. When he returned home, empty-handed, his children confronted him,

'Abba, did you find our mother?'

The father replied, 'No, I could not find her.'

The children were hard to pacify.

Lephai slept that night with a heavy heart, as he was very sad and worried.

The next day, he woke up and went again in the forest to look for his wife. He enquired many people if they had seen her or knew her whereabouts. Someone told Lephai that a fire was seen in the night on the top of the hill.

'Someone must be living there.'

'What is the name of that place?' Lephai enquired.

'Bontaing,' people told him.

He thought of visiting the place at night. He came back home and was confronted with the same question by his children.

'Father, did you find her?'

'No, I could not find her.' He replied gloomily.

As soon as the children went off to sleep, he left the house very quietly.

He went to the seaside and lowered the boat in the water. He started rowing the boat towards the place, where the locals had seen the fire. When he came near Bontaing, he saw the light of the burning fire. He waited till the fire got extinguished. 'It seems they have gone to sleep now,' he mumbled.

He stealthily approached the house and saw Noe sleeping with his wife. He was so outraged that initially, he thought of killing him outright.

'No, first, I will wake him up, and then I will kill him, so that he knows who killed him and why,' he thought.

Lephai then woke Noe up. As soon as Noe opened his eyes, he looked up and saw Lephai standing over him. Before he could rise, Lephai shot an arrow in his shoulder joint so that his arm got stuck as if it was stitched to his side. Immediately, he shot another arrow and hit his kneecap, restricting his movement completely. Noe fell down right there. In the meanwhile, Lephai's wife woke up and, seeing the whole scene, started to run. Lephai shot her immediately in the back, right where the arrow could pierce her heart. His wife fell on the ground and died immediately.

Lephai then went back to Noe and said, 'Why did you run away with her? Could you not find any woman in the world other than my wife? That is why I want to kill you. Little do you know with what difficulties I have raised my children. If you were in love with my wife, you should have told me earlier. Had you done that, I would never have married this girl.'

On hearing all this, Noe requested Lephai, 'Why don't you kill me right away? Why are you giving me this pain?'

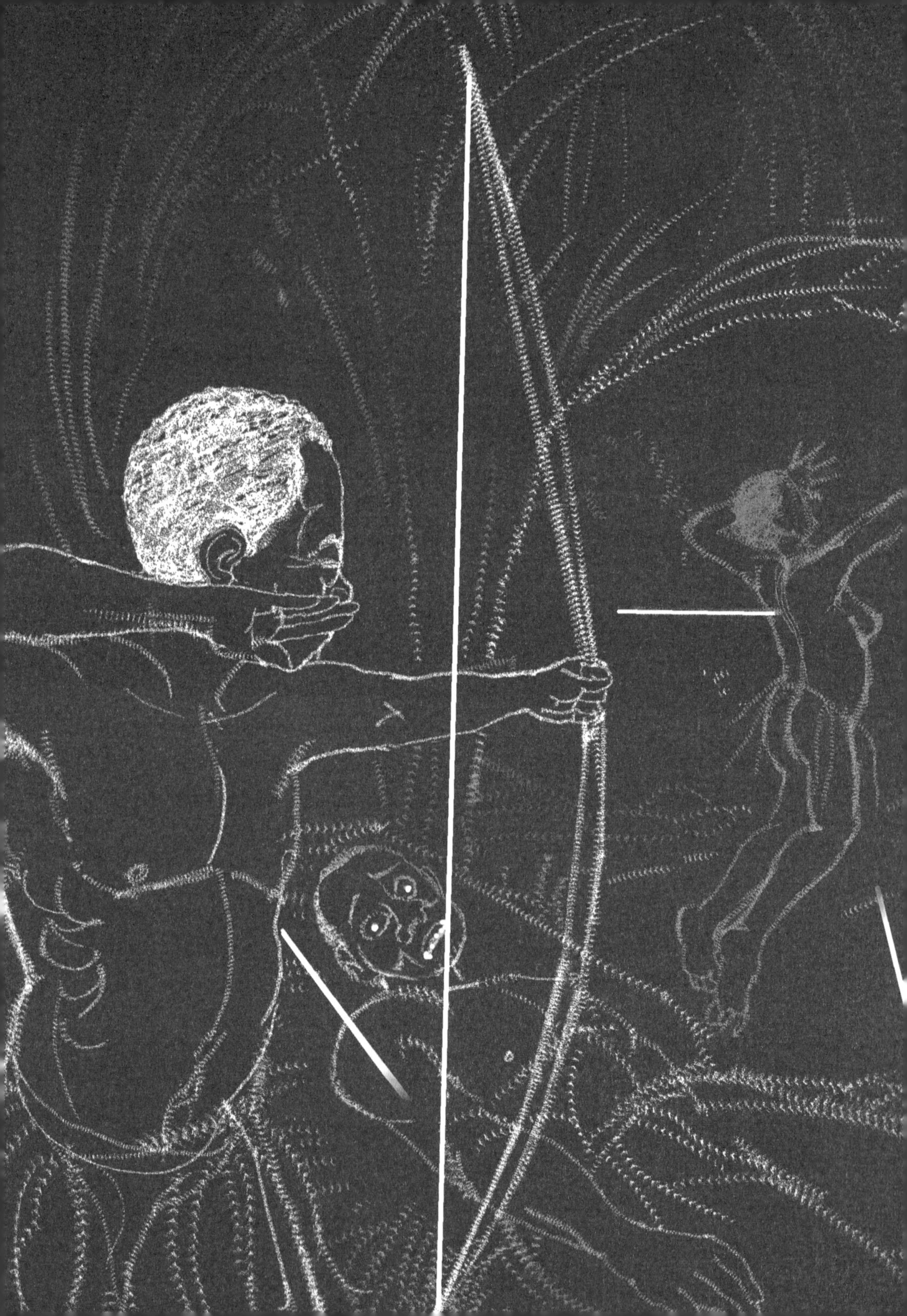

'Until I am finished talking to you and until I have emptied my heart, I shall not kill you. I will force you to suffer for some time.'

Lephai kept telling him his woes and when he had expressed his anger to his heart's content, he said, 'Now, I will kill you.' He drew a knife from his chest-guard and pierced it through Noe's heart.

Having taken revenge on Noe, Lephai then picked up his wife's body and laid her next to dead Noe. He broke down the thatch, cut up all the wooden walls, collected all the artifacts of the house, and piled up everything on the two bodies. Lephai then set the house on fire. He thus burned his wife and her lover.

Thereafter, he returned home. He was very sad and quiet. He had some plans, but dared not to discuss with anyone. He picked up his children and went deep into the forest of Bolphung. No one has seen Maya Lephai or his children ever since.

**

Note: The original version of the story with line-by-line translation in English is available in A2 of the Appendix.

Song 3: *aa jilap tara kamoo kamoonge erulu cholo chalo chalonge ee rulu cholo chalo chalonge ee rulu*
Meaning: Ah! Eyes aiming somewhere and glancing somewhere else! Glancing somewhere else, glancing somewhere else!
Singer: Boa Sr
Tribe: Bo
The song describes a young lover, bashful of the partner, stealing glances of the lover, while looking in a different direction to avoid direct eye contact.

Scan the QR code for the audio-visual recording of this song

Maya Jiro Mithe

Narrated by Nao Jr on 4 January 2007 in Port Blair

I was collecting the names of various endemic birds[16] from Nao, when I suddenly asked him, 'Don't you remember any story about birds?' He said he had heard one story, in which, all the Andamanese people became birds, but told me that he would have to think about it overnight to narrate it to me. I appreciated his willingness to help and we fixed a time to meet in the Circuit House on 4 January 2007 to record the story. Thus, was recorded the story of Jiro Mithe, one of my favourites. He was very happy that day as he could remember the story very well. He told me that he had been thinking of it all through the night. This was an unusual story, as the names of the various Andamanese birds are taken from the names of the Andamanese people, contrary to the general phenomenon, where the reverse is practised. Not only could he recollect what he had heard in his childhood, but he could also remember words for birds from his heritage language, which went a long way in helping me enrich the dictionary of Great Andamanese as well as identify each bird scientifically with the help of the ornithologist, Satish Pande. He would switch back and forth between Andamanese Hindi and Great Andamanese, like a perfect bilingual. In some

ways, I felt very proud of myself for having been able to help him revive the lost language.

Nao often used to interrupt his narratives with observations on the depleting population of the Great Andamanese tribe, for instance, 'There were many people at that time. No one is left now.' I heard him lamenting in Hindi, 'Koi nahin bachaa.' He once said that the names of the birds are so many because they were transformed from human beings—a myth that most of the tribes believe in. I was surprised at the logistics. Photographs of some of the common birds with their Andamanese names are given in this book.

It is a kind of creation myth, which informs us of the evolution of birds and their distinct and varied names. After listening to this story, I understood why birds are considered the ancestors of the Andamanese.[17] This is a story of a boy, who belonged to the Jero tribe, the tribe that lived near the seashore. Other tribes who lived near the seashore were Khora, Bo, and Sare. This story tells of the man, who was swallowed by a Bol fish and then all the rescuers became birds.

THE STORY OF MAYA JIRO MITHE

Jiro Mithe was a young boy from the Jero tribe who was very fond of hunting in the sea. Once he went hunting in the sea, but could not find anything. Later on, he found a muscle like fish, *khata*, a squid. He sat down by the seashore to clean it. The more he cleaned it, the bigger it became. Finally, Jiro Mithe swallowed the whole *khata* as he could not wait to eat it. While cleaning the *khata* and swallowing it, he had been sitting in a crouching position.

Suddenly a big fish, a *bol*[18], came to the shore and swallowed the crouching Mithe. He was unaware of his surroundings. He wondered where he was, as he could not recognize this new place, that is, inside the stomach of the *bol* fish. He could not even move his limbs as the place was rather tight and slimy.

Jiro Mithe's family was worried, as no one had seen him for one or two days. His folks went to the seashore and found the remains of the *khata* and knew that this must have been the job of Jiro Mithe. They also found his bow and arrow lying on the shore and knew immediately that Mithe had not gone for hunting.

'Where can he go?' someone asked.

'He must be somewhere nearby,' another said.

After searching for a long time, Mithe was nowhere to be traced. His folks thought, 'He must have been eaten by the *bol*.'

The folks started their journey into the sea to hunt for the *bol*. They knew that the *bol* could not have gone too far, as his stomach was full of Mithe. Soon, they saw traces of dirty water in the sea.

'See the dirty line that the Bol fish has left behind,' Phatka said.

'Yes, we can trace its track,' Kaulo said. Benge nodded in agreement.

As Phatka was the cleverest of all, he was asked to trace the *bol* fish. Phatka went further into the sea. Soon Phatka found the fish with a bulging belly. All could see Mithe still sitting in a crouched position inside.

Phatka tried to kill the fish with a long bamboo, but it would not reach the *bol*. Benge also tried, but did not succeed. Finally, they agreed that this job can only be accomplished by Kaulo, and they began calling out for him, 'Kauloooo….'

Kaulo had gone in the sea on a boat to look for Jiro Mithe. He heard the voices of Benge and Phatka. 'Oh, they must have found Mithe,' he thought and started rowing his boat towards them.

'Where is he?' Kaulo asked.

'Here he is, here he is,' they replied.

Kaulo said, 'Look for the fish's head, it must be in the sand.'

All the folks saw it clearly. The head of the fish was hidden in the sand. Kaulo said, 'We have to hit him on the head and nowhere else, because if we hit him in the belly, then Mithe will be hurt.'

'We found it, we found it!' they yelled, as they detected the fish's head in the sand.

Kaulo hit the head of bol hard. As soon as he hit him, the fish started to swim away, as fast as it could.

Kaulo ordered everyone to tie their boats with ropes, so that the fish could not overturn them and could also be hunted easily. He threw one rope towards the fish to snare him and then jabbed it with poles and a harpoon. Thus, the bol was killed.

'Tie the fish to the side of the boat and pull him to the shore,' Kaulo instructed. His folks did as they were told. They all brought the fish to the seashore and, with great care, cut his belly with the knife that Kaulo had.

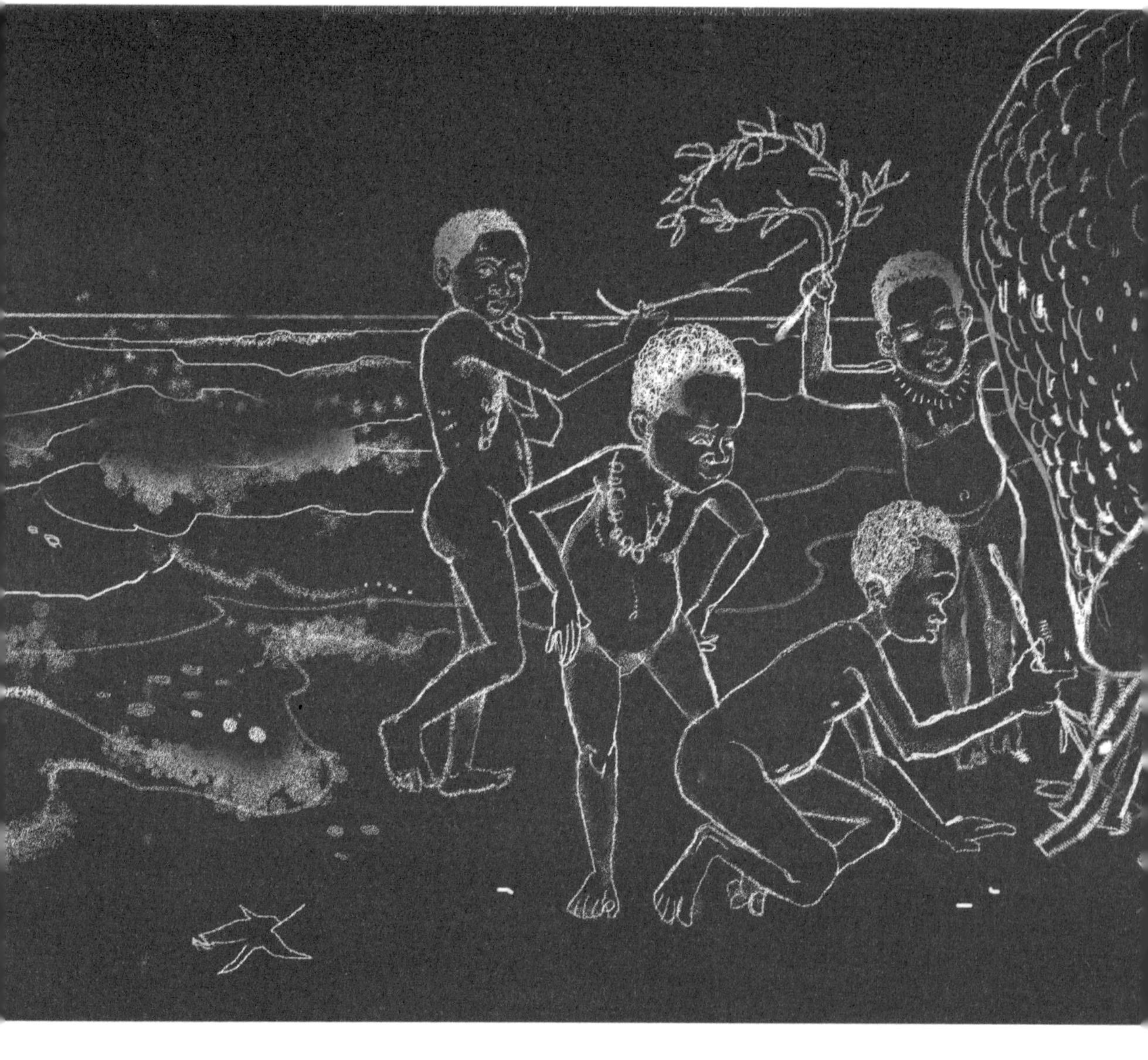

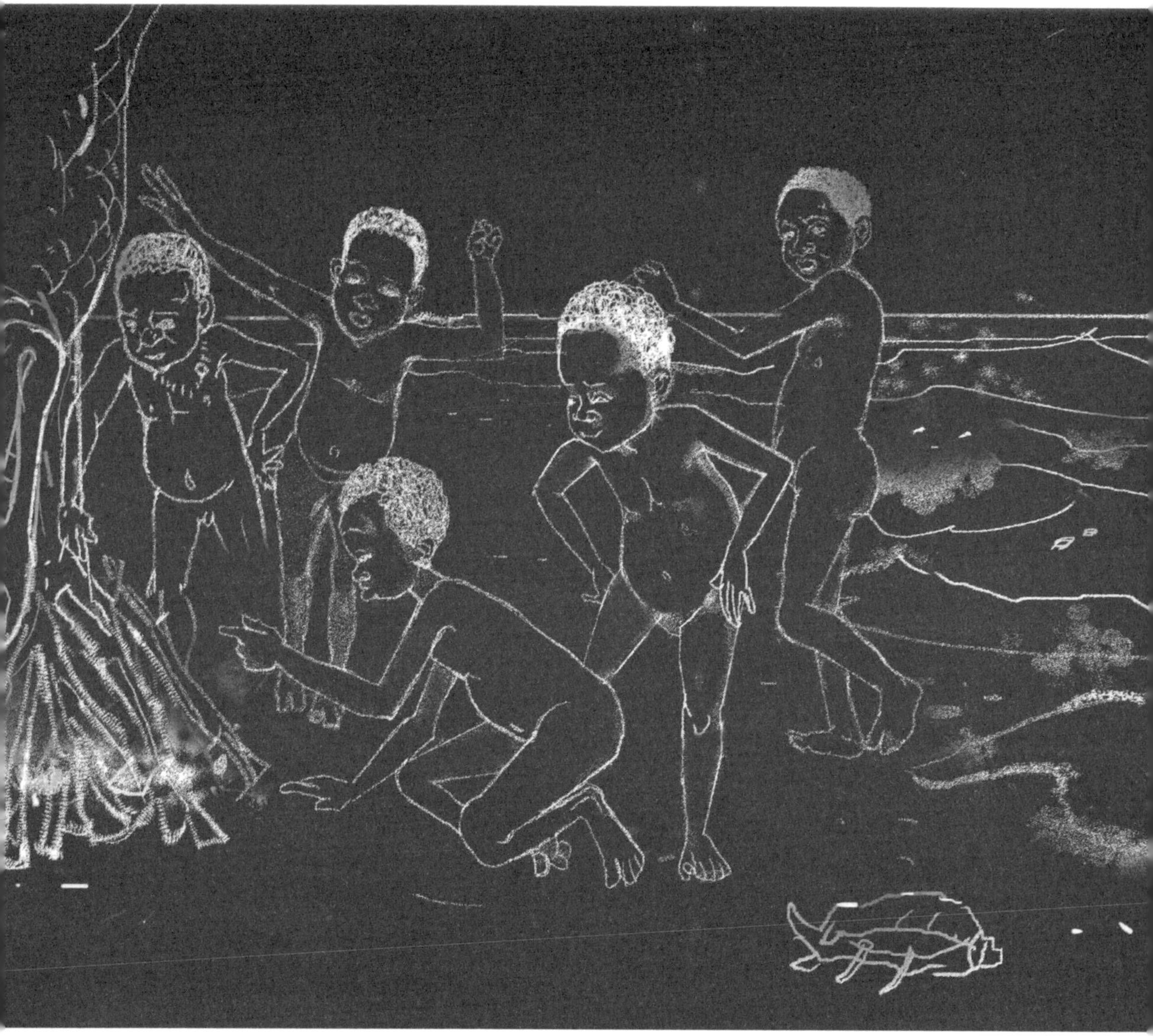

Mithe came out alive, but he was still sitting in a crouching position. His limbs had got numb and soft as he had been squeezed in the stomach of the *bol* for a very long time.

Everyone helped to prepare a *machaan* or a raised platform and lit a fire under it, so that Mithe's limbs could be warmed. After Mithe was feeling better, one of them asked,

'How will we eat the *bol*?'

'We will cut it up in small pieces and then roast the pieces in the fire on the *machaan*,' someone suggested.

And that is what was done. Each of them cut the huge fish into small pieces. Only the children were left behind. Kaulo's children said,

'Abba, once you cut the fish into pieces, give them to us, so that we can cook them in the fire.'

The children started making a lot of noise. Some started howling. On hearing their constant demand, Kaulo got very angry, but did cut up the fish into small pieces for his children. The children went towards the raised platform and threw them in the fire to roast.

When the pieces started getting roasted, one of them (known as *totale*[19]) kept swelling like a tummy. It kept on increasing in length too as if it was made of a rubber-like structure. It became longer and longer and longer....

Kaulo and his folks were so engrossed in cutting the rest of the fish that they did not notice the swelling of the *totale*. Nor Kaulo knew that a fish's *totale* was not support to be put on fire.

Suddenly, the *totale* burst with a big noise, and all the folks, including the children, became birds.

Kaulo looked back and realized all the children had become small birds and flown to the sky.

He himself had become a bird.

He looked at the *machaan*, but could not find Mithe. Mithe too had become a bird.

If the children had not cooked the *totale*, everyone would have been saved. But now, all of them had become birds.

Since then, we do not kill *bol* fish. And the names of our Andamanese birds are Kaulo, Phatka, Benge, Bemokatap, Balatbai, Chelene, and Mithe.

***

Note: The original story with line-by-line translation in English is available in A3 of the Appendix.

Song 4: *ngercho tuloe chong chiri chiri ngercho tuloe chong chiri chiri*
Meaning: A bird with a big beak is searching something here and there.
Singer: Boa Sr
Tribe: Bo
This song by Boa Sr is about a bird that is searching for food here and there with its beak. Boa Sr used to talk to birds as she believed that they understood her language Bo. Birds in Great Andamanese are considered to be their ancestors. Read the story 'Maya Jiro Mithe'.

Scan the QR code for the audio-visual recording of this song

75

Birds in Great Andamanese nomenclature are often given names where each has an underlying meaning, as you will observe in the story above.
Here are some birds with their Great Andamanese names.
Sources: *Birds of the Great Andamanese*

Koi, the Andaman Woodpecker

Bemokatap, the Andaman Bulbul

Phatka, the Indian Crow

Taitpheno, the White-breasted Kingfisher

Bolmikhu, the Stork-billed Kingfisher

Cereo, the Asian Koel (male)

Cereo, the Asian Koel (female)

Balatbai, the Andaman Drongo

Milidu, the Nicobar Pigeon

Mithe, the Andaman Cuckoo Dove

Benge, the Andaman Serpent Eagle

Chelene, the Crab Plover

Kala Top, the Hermit Crab

Kaulo, the White-bellied Sea Eagle

Phuro, the Andaman Owl

Kaliu, the Common Hill Myna

Lacha, the Black-naped Tern

Toromtubiyo, the Red Munia

Taka, the Pacific Reef Heron

Dik and Kaunmo

Narrated by Nao Jr on 4 January 2007 in Port Blair

*O*n the same day when Nao narrated to me the story of Jiro Mithe, that is, 4 January 2007, Nao narrated another story, the story of 'Dik and Kaunmo', the evil man and his wife. Initially, he was a little hesitant to tell the story, but I requested him to be comfortable. He said, 'This is a story I feel shy telling in front of a lady.' When I persuaded him to shed away any inhibition that he might have had on my account, he began narrating. I had thought that the story might have sexual overtones, but it was funny and a little gross, as it mentioned farting several times. He laughed heartily while rendering the Great Andamanese words 'thure thure' ('aroma aroma') repeatedly, as he found it very funny. When I asked him why Dik's wife behaved so badly with him, prompt came the reply, 'For the sake of her children. Dik never bothered about his wife or the children.' He further explained, 'When the wife asked him to take the children along with him (to the seashore), he would not listen to her. She was heartbroken.'

Nao surprised me with his sophisticated behaviour, unparalleled by any other person I met on the Islands. I would not have been surprised, if educated and intellectual Indians would think twice before narrating a *story like 'Dik and Kaumno' in front of a lady. The demeanour that Nao showed left me appreciative of his tribe, his upbringing. Nao was also very proud of his heritage and his upbringing.*

THE STORY OF DIK AND KAUNMO

Once there was a man called Dik, who had a wife named Kaunmo. Kaunmo did not like her husband at all, because he was an evil man. From time to time, he would thrash her. He would also beat and trouble their children. Moreover, Dik never provided for the children. So, Kaunmo had to work very hard to gather and hunt food for her several children. She had to walk far to fetch drinking

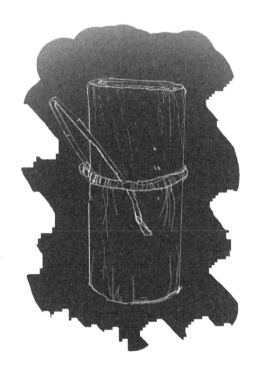

water from the river in the hollows of big bamboos and in wooden baskets. She toiled all day long, but Dik would not help her in any of the chores.

She would spread big leaves and serve meat pieces for her children. Dik would pounce on them and gobble them up, never sparing any for the others. Such was his appetite!

One afternoon, when Dik was sleeping, she asked her children to eat lots of potatoes as they produce acidity and gas in the stomach. The children followed their mother's advice. When their stomachs were full, she asked them to go to their father, one by one.

She told them to fart right on his nose as hard as they could.

The children did exactly as they were told, but no one's fart was loud enough to wake Dik up.

Their mother Kaunmo said, 'You people are good for nothing. Let me try.'

She went up to her sleeping husband and farted as loud as she could right on his nose.

This sound was loud enough to break his slumber.

Dik woke up saying, '*Thure thure* (wonderful smell, wonderful smell)!'

Such were the ways Kaunmo used to show her dissatisfaction with her husband.

As the years passed, Dik's behaviour towards his children and wife worsened.

One fine day, when Dik was sleeping by the sea, on the sand, Kaunmo collected several black poisonous sea urchins and spread them all around him.

As Dik turned his side while sleeping, all the sea urchins pierced his body. He cried in pain and turned the other side. But the other side of his body only got pierced by more sea urchins, as his wife had spread them all around him. At last, in deep pain, Dik tried to get up and several sea urchins further pierced his bottom. There was just no respite. Dik wriggled and wriggled in pain till he died. He thus met his end at the hands of his wife.

✳✳✳

Note: Andaman sea urchin, *moroi*, is a black poisonous sea organism that has innumerable thorns on its body like a porcupine. A slight contact with this may cause pain for days. Once the thorn is pierced in the body, it is sure to bring death.

Song 5: *dol koṟonge ṭonge jara taikhdunya ila do jara taikhdunya, ila do jara taikh dunya, ila do jara taikhdunya*
Meaning: The Earth is shaking as the tree falls with a great thud.
Singer: Boa Sr
Tribe: Bo
In this song, Boa Sr describes vividly the day tsunami approached the island on 26 December 2004. She says that trees were falling with a loud noise and the earth was shaking vigorously. She told us that the ancestors had told her that when earth shakes, one should take a bamboo and hit the earth several times to stop it from shaking.

Scan the QR code for the audio-visual recording of this song

Golat and Tae Daniel

The Story of Two Brothers and a Crocodile

Narrated by Nao Jr on 5 January 2007, Port Blair

*A*mong all the Andamanese tribes that Nao knew, he considered the Pujjukars the strongest. Pujjukars lived on the western side of the Great Andaman. He would never tire telling stories of their valour and fearlessness. He once narrated a story of two brothers, Tae Daniel and Golat, who were captured by the British soldiers and were kept in the Port Blair jail. Nao told me in detail how Golat broke all the iron chains and ran away from the jail to take refuge in the sea. Golat was known to be a friend of a crocodile, as he was often seen riding the crocodile's head in the sea and the swamps. I could not believe these stories, but he pledged time and again that these were not fiction, but true stories. The Pujjukars are known to be violent and hot-headed as there are several stories involving their fights with the crocodile with bare hands. He thought even the British feared the Pujjukars. Interestingly, one of the speakers of the current language, Licho, a female in her mid-fifties was brought up by a Pujjukar elder. Nao always believed that the tribes living in the North Sentinel Islands were Pujjukars too, as they were strong and courageous, who had so far resisted any outside intervention.

Meeting Licho and her family, Port Blair; at the extreme right is Pramod Kumar (December 2001)

THE STORY OF GOLAT AND TAE DANIEL

This is the story of two Pujjukar brothers, Golat and Tae Daniel, who belonged to the Bie tribe. Golat was very strong. Once upon a time, the two brothers were playing in the shallow water of the sea when a crocodile swallowed Tae Daniel. Seeing this, Golat mounted the crocodile and rode on his head for almost a month and a half. Wherever the crocodile went, Golat would go along with him riding on his head. He would travel to marshes in the bay, near the mangroves and by the seashore. He was protected by the 'jurwachom'[20] in the sea, and thus the crocodile could not harm him. However, this did not last long. For some time later, a duel between the crocodile and Golat began. No one knows why and how a duel started between the two.

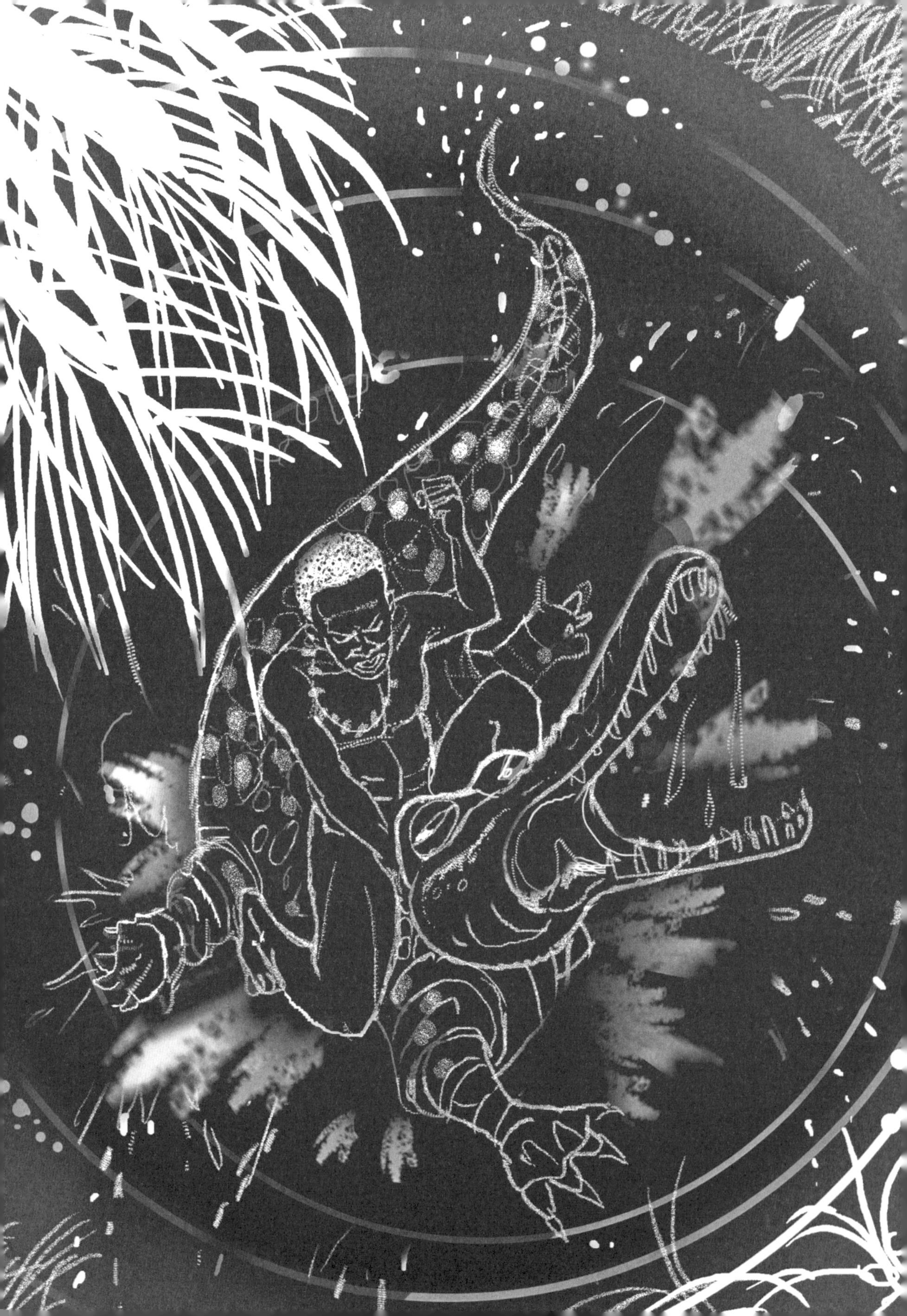

But it is believed that Golat forced the crocodile to go into the marshes, because he knew that in the marshes, the strength of crocodiles gets quickly worn away. This leaves them too weak to attack. On reaching such marshy a land, he fought with the crocodile with his bare hands. So strong was Golat that he broke all the four legs of the crocodile. This made walking difficult for the creature. The crocodile could no longer hunt in the bay and thus met his end. Seeing this sad state of affairs, the other crocodiles did not leave Golat alone and killed him. Surprisingly, they did not eat him up.

Our folks who go fishing in the bay in their *dongi*s found Golat's body. They also spotted the marks of the fight between the crocodile and Golat under the seabed. They also found the dead body of the crocodile with cut-up legs.

This is a true story of valour of a Pujjukar boy, Golat.

Song 6: *lele phurjole ṭokhat korme lele*
Meaning: I swing your cradle of bamboo back and
forth, back and forth
Singer: Boa Sr
Tribe: Bo
This is a rare lullaby in Great Andamanese which describes
the to-and-fro motion of a bamboo cradle. Unfortunately,
lullabies are lost to the community and at present, most
Andamanese mothers put their babies to sleep without
humming any lullaby.

Scan the QR code
for the audio-visual
recording of this song

Maya Boro and Jurwachom

The Story of a Man with Supernatural Powers

As told by Nao Jr on 5 January 2007

*A*nother story by the name of Maya Boro and Jurwachom exposed me to their supernatural beliefs. As said earlier, the word 'maya' in Great Andamanese means 'late' or 'ancient'. The naming system of the Great Andamanese tribe is not gender-specific as the name of a child is given when it is in the womb. Thus, a name like 'Boro' or 'Nao' could be either given to a male or a female child. Moreover, the name of a child changes four times in a life span depending upon the various stages of life he or she goes through. The last stage is when the person leaves this world and becomes 'Maya' which is prefixed to the same name that was given to her/him when s/he was in the womb of her/his mother. 'Maya Boro and Jurwachom is a story that was narrated to Nao by Moroi, the father of Nao Jr when Nao was a child. Nao said that he remembered Boro, his grandfather, and was convinced that Boro had some supernatural powers. Nao reported this as a true incident that took place not very long ago, perhaps 70 years ago. The mention of the dog, pipe, tobacco, and tea leaves in the story certainly indicates its recent origin, to the time when India was ruled by the British. This also implies that cannibalism did exist until very recently, though it is *always despised in the stories. The character of Jurwachom seems very interesting as the so-called 'devils of the sea and the jungle' were kind and helpful to the protagonist of the story, yet they practise cannibalism and offer human flesh to Boro for consumption. I have retained the first-person narrative here to maintain authenticity.*

THE STORY OF MAYA BORO AND JURWACHOM

Maya Boro was an elderly man, perhaps the oldest in the community. He was gifted with supernatural powers. Many of us considered him mad. He was married to Tango. They had no children of their own, but they loved others' children, especially my father, Maroi[21]. Boro had a dog too. This is a story of the time when my father was young…perhaps 13 or 14 years old.

Boro had the habit of taking an afternoon nap. He never liked to be disturbed, while he took his afternoon siesta. He would always tell his wife that neither she nor any child should disturb him while he was taking a nap. He said that *motkochup* or 'heavenly bodies' came and rested on the peepal tree. 'They talk to me while I am asleep. I won't like to be disturbed.' He would instruct her thus: 'You don't wake me up, I will get up on my own.'

In his dream, he would wish for various things. And when he woke up, those things would be found by his side. He used to wish for tea leaves, tobacco, etc. His wife was always amazed and used to wonder where he got these things from.

After his siesta, he would ask his wife Tango to check his armpit. When she touched his armpit, she would sometimes find a packet of

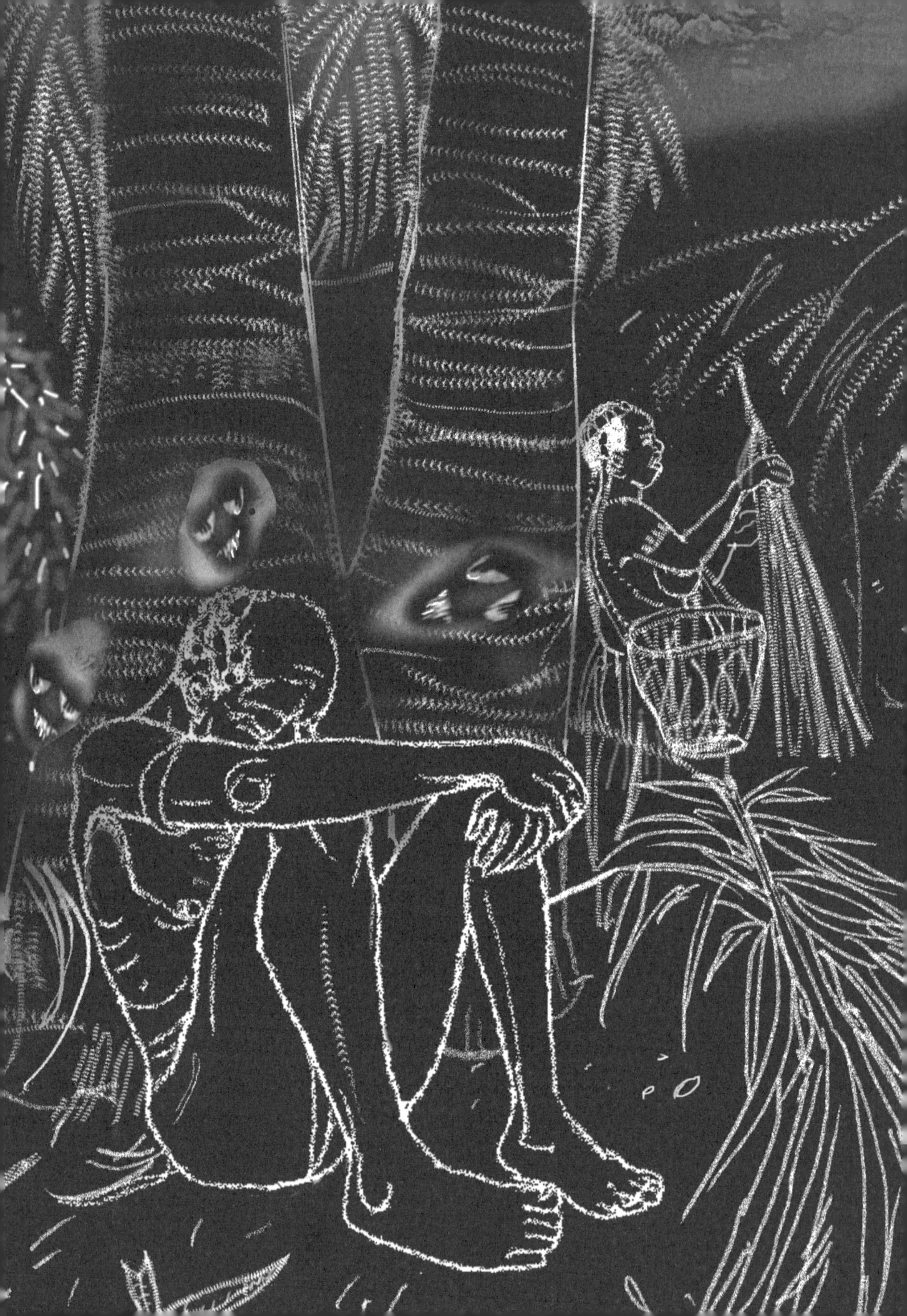

tea leaves or at others, dry tobacco leaves, tucked in. He would fill the tobacco leaves in the hollow of the crab's legs, *phong toy*, and smoke it like a pipe imitating the Europeans. He could repeat this magic again and again to the utter surprise of his wife.

One fine day, Boro took my father to the jungle for hunting. They hunted so much that they wondered how they would carry all that game home. Boro told my father to pick up only two of the animals, and he decided to carry the rest. When my father carried the two animals, a strange thing happened. He did not feel the weight at all, as if he was carrying something very light.

After reaching home, they cut up the pieces of the hunted boars and distributed the meat in the colony, so that everyone could have a feast.

After this episode, he would, now and then, call my father, as he was very fond of him, and ask him to accompany him to the sea. My father would say,

'No, I do not want to go with an old man.'

To this, Boro would say, 'Who is the old man here? I am a child yet.'

My father would laugh and go along. On one such escapade, while my father was standing by the seashore, Boro sat at the head of the *dongi*, smoking his crab pipe. He threw out a challenge that even if he got into the water, the fire in the pipe would not extinguish. My father said, 'Show me,' and Boro obliged him by turning the boat upside down in water, emerging again with a smoke-emitting pipe. He repeated this magic several times to my father's astonishment. My father thought that if he performed the same exercise, perhaps, he could also attain the same results.

He said, 'Well, I can also do that!'

'Try it.' Boro said, 'I am sure when you do it, the fire in the pipe will go out.'

My father mounted the boat and turned the boat upside down and when he emerged on the surface of the water, the fire in the pipe was no more to be seen. He was disappointed.

'How did you do that?' My father asked.

'I will teach you,' Boro said.

'Well, there are *jurowachom*, devils, under the sea who help me protect the fire in the pipe.'

'Who are *jurwachom*?' my father asked.

'They are devils who live in the water by the seashore and eat human flesh.'

'How do they protect your pipe?'

'Well, when I go down, they put their hand on my pipe, so no water goes in and, when I come up, they remove their hand,' Boro explained.

My father was scared to death hearing that and asked no more.

One fine day, Boro brought lots of pig's meat and asked my father to cut it up in pieces. He did as he was told. My father was then asked to boil the meat. My father boiled it all in a big pot. Boro heaped all those boiled pieces in several plates. The plates were full. I remember my father telling us that he never saw so much meat on one plate ever again in his life. That night, my father, as usual, was asked to accompany Boro into the forest. It was a dark night and the forest was dense. My father was scared. He could not see anything.

'I feel scared,' my father told Boro.

'Why?' Boro asked him.

'I am afraid of the darkness,' my father said.

'Don't be afraid,' Boro assured my father.

Boro asked him to hold on to his *arabel* or waistband, made of seashells. Though he was still scared, my father held on to Boro's arabel and followed him into the forest.

Once they had reached deep inside the forest, Boro said, 'Halt! I will call the *jurwachom*[22].'

He called them twice, but no response came. He called them again, and this time my father could hear voices, as if some people were talking and laughing. When he tried to see in the dark, he could not see anything. It was pitch dark. Boro served the heaps of meat on the plates he had brought along. My father could hear sounds of enjoyment, of people fighting over a piece of flesh or bone, of laughing, chewing, gnawing, and eating of the meat. But he could not see a thing. Soon, he realized that the plates were empty. He moved his hands around the plates, thinking perhaps, the meat pieces had fallen down. But no, there was not a morsel. He was amazed to see how soon so much meat could disappear.

Out of gratitude, *jurwachom* gifted a big piece of human flesh to Boro. He and my father returned home after this episode.

Once they reached home, Boro cut up the meat into several small pieces and asked my father to eat. My father did not know that it was human flesh, though he suspected it to be so. He tried to eat it, but could not. As soon as a piece of meat would go down his throat, he would choke. My father could not swallow it despite several attempts.

In fact, he vomited everything out. It is said that my father, since this episode, lost his hearing power. Boro told him that if he had been able to eat it and digest it, nothing of this sort would have happened.

***

Note: This is a story that was narrated by Moroi, the father of Nao Jr when Nao was a child. Nao Jr had seen Boro in his life and was convinced that Boro had some supernatural powers.

Song 7: *ankile ṭima erachong me ṭorola ai ḍabegri, larola ai ḍabegri, larola ai*
Meaning: This is a chant by a boat maker who seeks divine blessings, so that he can build a canoe well to face the rough sea.
Singer: Boa Sr
Tribe: Bo

Scan the QR code for the audio-visual recording of this song

Dik, the Demon, and the Fish

Narrated by Boa Sr in December 2005

*T*here is only one story in this collection, which is not narrated by Nao. The short story of 'Dik the Demon' was narrated to us by the eldest member of the community, Boa Sr about 80 years old and popularly known as 'chaachii', the Hindi word for 'aunt'. Though she kept saying that she had forgotten all the stories she had ever heard in her childhood, yet after many visits to her little cottage and several requests, she obliged us finally with the story of 'Dik the Demon'. Perhaps it was possible for her to recollect the events of the story as the hiding place of the fish and the famous rock still existed in Mayabandar, the place she spent all her life before she was resettled on Strait Island in the '70s. When one is forcibly uprooted from one's home, one tends to lose interest in the present life, but relives the past over and over again. She was the only member of the community and had no one of her own. She never had any children. All her relatives were gone, yet her full-throated laugh was infectious. I vividly remember that Boa Sr could never complete a sentence without a hearty laugh. An ever-smiling lady, she missed Mayabandar so much that no incident or visit was without a mention of her life at Mayabandar, the north of the Andaman Islands. Later, I realized that she did not share

Boa Sr with the author in her cottage at Strait Island (December 2005)

her past life with anyone else in the community as no one among the existing people came from the same place. We were, perhaps, the only ones who were interested in her past. Her narration, though minimal, was so vivid that I was tempted to visit the place and see the rocks mentioned in the current tale.

THE STORY OF DIK THE DEMON AND THE FISH

Our elders told us several stories of our ancient people. There used to be different kinds of people in the world. They used to live near our ancient abode, Diglipur. They are no more to be seen anywhere. I wonder where they have all gone!

Dik was a demon but looked like a human. He was larger than the big trees growing around Diglipur. Dik had a special gift of being able to walk on the surface of the water. He was the only one who could walk on water.

Once he saw a very big fish. He wanted to catch it. As the fish was moving very fast ahead of him, he started chasing it and thus did not realize that he had come very far from home. The fish, while trying to escape from Dik, crashed against a rock near Interview Island. A big hole was formed in the rock by the impact. The fish took refuge inside the rock. The rock still bears the sign of the fish banging into it.

Chasing the fish, Dik reached the rock, but he could not see the fish. 'Where did it go?'

Then he saw the tail of the fish jutting out of the hole of the rock. He brought a rope and tied the tail with the rope. Then he pulled the fish out.

Once out of the hill-cave, the fish started again to try to escape, but could not succeed. Dik killed the fish with his arrow. The fish died. The fish *tumunye* was huge. The fat alone of the *tumunye* could fill up several bowls.

Dik was no less dangerous himself. He was a headhunter and used to eat humans. Because of this reason, his children had abandoned him. He was lonely and desolate. Later, our ancestors killed him. He is not seen any more these days.

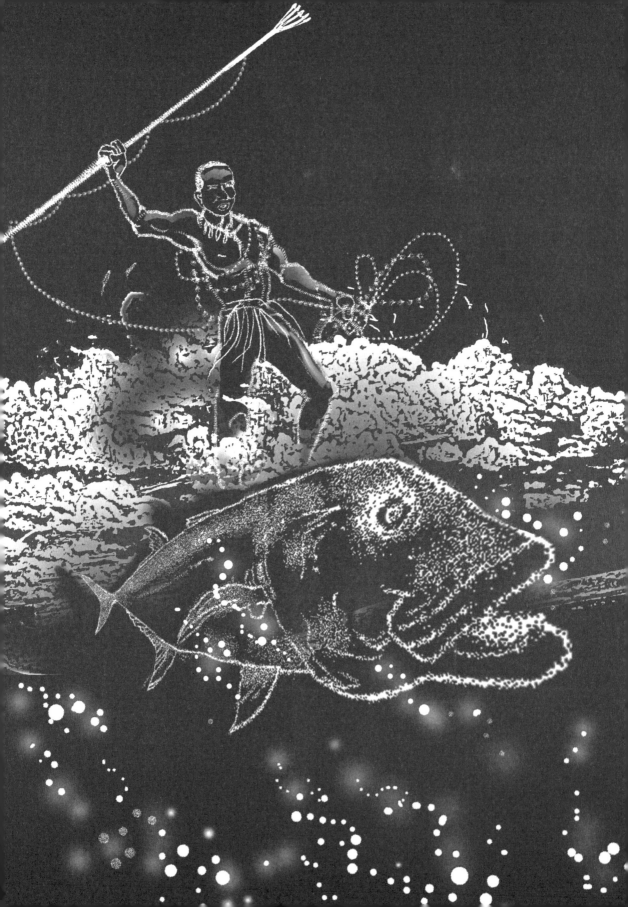

Note: We are not sure whether this Dik and the one in the tale of Dik with Kaunmo is the same person. However, there are many similarities in the personalities of the two. On the other hand, Dik is a generic name for 'demon' and hence, these two Diks could be different persons. This was another story where we found the reference of cannibalism as well, although looked down upon by the society.

Song 8: *teri dongathe balau kulti bangau teri dongathe*
Meaning: Children are unable to reach up to the fruits on the tree as they are quite high up.
Singer: Boa Sr
Tribe: Bo

Scan the QR code
for the audio-visual
recording of this song

The Water God Maya-Kobo and Jire

Narrated by Nao Jr on 29 December 2006

VERSION I

Nao once told me an interesting story where the protagonist curses his attacker. Till then I did not know that the act of cursing could be found in an ancient civilization. The Great Andamanese people love hunting turtles and even now the elders describe in detail how the turtle is hunted, then roasted on stone, and distributed piece by piece in the entire village. One finds various sizes of turtles in the Andaman sea; small ones, which they call 'toro', and very large ones such as Leatherbacks are known as 'cokbi'. The present story appears to be the story of Leatherback. This story was narrated in Hindi by Nao and later, on my insistence, he went through the journey of reverse translation and many times adding the original thoughts in the Andamanese language and thus, we obtained the story in the heritage language. It was noticed that he was not fluent as can be seen by his short sentences, but the process of language revival was evident. One can read the story in the original in the appendix (A4).

THE STORY OF MAYA-KOBO AND JIRE

Now I tell you the story of Maya-Kobo and Jire.

Maya-Kobo was sleeping on an ancient turtle in the sea. He used to sleep on the turtle and even his wife was instructed not to wake him up when he slept like this. The turtle he used to sleep on was no ordinary turtle. He was like our forefathers. Maya-Kobo was an omniscient being, one who could discern others' secret desires.

Jire was a young boy who was a good hunter. Once he went hunting with his friends for turtles at night, because it is easy to hunt them in the dark. At night, turtles swim on the surface of the water and thus can be easily spotted. That night, Jire hunted many turtles. Unfortunately, quite inadvertently, one of Jire's *roy*s (harpoons) hit Maya-Kobo's head. It went through and through his forehead.

After being hit by Jire, Maya-Kobo returned home and told his wife, 'Jire hit me in the head, while I was lying on the back of the ancient turtle. Go and tell this to his parents. He must be approaching the shore now. You can hear the sounds of the boat.'

As soon as Jire's parents heard this, they got worried, because they knew that Maya-Kobo would not spare their son's life. Maya-Kobo put a curse on Jire pronouncing that he would die soon.

As soon as he was cursed by Maya-Kobo, Jire started feeling nauseous. He could no longer pull the rope of the *roy*. He asked his friends to help him pull the rope. He said, 'I am feeling giddy and nauseous.' As soon as he reached the shore, he collapsed on the ground and died. Jire's life ended thus, because of the curse of Maya-Kobo, who was himself suffering from the wound inflicted on him by Jire. Maya-Kobo was sure to die, as the wound was right on his forehead.

Maya-Kobo's wife could not believe that her husband was hurt in the brain and was going to die. Maya-Kobo tried to convince his wife that after he was buried in the earth, she should dig up his grave after a few days to confirm that he was indeed shot in the brain.

After the death of Maya-Kobo, he was buried in the earth. After some time, his wife dug up the grave and sure enough, she found her husband's skull had a hole through and through. She noticed a little blood around the hole too. She was now convinced that her husband was killed in the head by Jire.

Since then, no one goes out at night to hunt turtles.

VERSION 2

Another version of the same story was narrated by Boa Sr, the last speaker of Bo, one of the 10 languages of the Great Andamanese language family.

Boa Sr could not render it in her native language. She used Andamanese Hindi. We are giving the English translation only.

THE STORY OF THE WATER GOD MAYA-KOBO AND JIRE

Even in ancient times, people would go turtle-hunting. They used to go during the day, as well as in the night. At night, as turtles move on the surface of the water, they are easy prey. Maya-Kobo is the water god. He walks on the surface of the water during the night. He takes care of all the animals in the water and is known as their protector.

There was a boy named Jire. He went turtle-hunting with his friends in the night. It was a dark night. He was rowing in the sea. He saw several creatures in the water, though nothing was visible very clearly. However, he could guess the presence of several turtles around.

He shot arrows all around him in the dark and caught several of the turtles. But one of the arrows hit the water god, Maya-Kobo. The arrow struck his forehead and went through and through. The blood oozed out and started flowing heavily. Because it was dark, Jire could not see that he had hit the water god. In sheer anger and desperation, Maya-Kobo cursed Jire to meet his end soon.

While Jire and his friends were coming back to the shores with the turtles, Jire felt dizzy and nauseous. Jire could not understand why he was suffering like this. Anyway, they came ashore. As soon as Jire got down from the canoe, he fell on the ground. He died instantly.

Since then, people do not go for hunting during the night.

**

Note: The original version with line-by-line translation in English is available in A4 of the Appendix.

Song 9: *dudama kuailang ijokongterbiroe dudama kuailarang lodopui jaga terenglo haludapui terenglo haludapui jaga terenglo haludapui jaga terenglo*
Meaning: Pull it to the shores. Turn over the catch. Turn over the catch quickly!!
Singer: Pa-Aung (Pao Buddha)
Tribe: Karen
This is a turtle-hunting song. The singer is asking his friend that the turtle should be brought to the shores and turned upside down quickly so that it cannot run away. The singer was in his 80s when I recorded this song. He is the only person in the island who learnt the Great Andamanese language as the second language from Nao Jr's father and remembers this song till today.

Scan the QR code for the audio-visual recording of this song

When We Hunted Dugong: A real story

Narrated by Nao Jr on 1 January 2007
Port Blair

*S*uddenly, Nao Jr became aware of the lost world that he had ceased to live in. It was his sheer desire to relive and experience his good old days, when his Abba (his father) or grandfather used to take him for hunting in the jungle or the sea. When he travelled in his boat in the middle of the night to hunt for dugong, he often witnessed the sparkle and the shimmering streak of light emitting from the sides of the dugong, swimming fast in the seawater. There were times when the dugong hit the boat from below and it split it into two parts, with him lying with his mother on one, while his Abba on the other, trying to save the remains of the boat in the moonlit night. This narration reflects a true event that took place in his life. It is heartening to watch how the last speakers of a language realize the imminent death of their language and thus, want to revive it at any cost, provided there is someone to listen to them. The following story was told to me twice—once in the heritage language and when not satisfied fully with the version—once again in the Andamanese variety of Hindi. The original version with line-by-line English translation is given in the appendix (A5). The running translation *appears in the following pages. The current story is proof of the love for hunting in the sea by the Great Andamanese tribe.*

THE STORY OF HUNTING DUGONG

'Loka was the name of my mother. One fine night, my father took Loka and me for hunting in the sea. For a while, he did not find any game. We noticed that there was another boat in the waters beside ours, hunting in the sea. Suddenly, we all saw a dugong. It was glowing underwater. We hit the creature. In retaliation, the dugong went around our boat and then started running backwards. My father was surprised by his action. Suddenly, the dugong hit our boat from the bottom in the centre. I was sleeping at the back of the boat and my

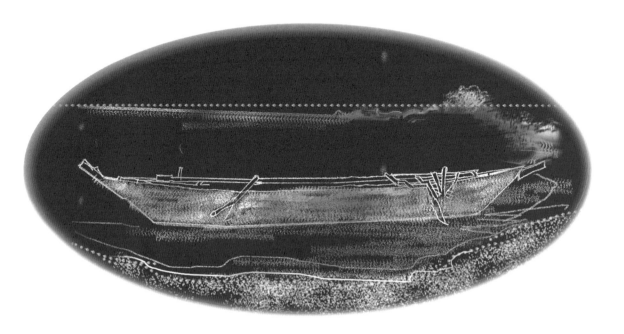

mother was rowing it. The dugong hit the boat so hard that it split into two pieces. I was with my mother, but my father got separated. He was on the other half of the boat. He shouted for help, but we could not comprehend what was going on. We were all taken by surprise. It was very dark. Mother then called for the other boat, which was rowing along with ours earlier. Hearing her voice, the other boat came near us. My mother and I mounted the other boat and went ahead looking for my father. We kept shouting for him and then we saw him right there in the middle of the sea. When we approached him, he climbed aboard. Thereafter, he untied the rope (as a dugong is always killed with a spear, which has a hook with a long rope) and jumped into the sea to tie the rope to the side of the boat. Thereafter, he hit the dugong in its armpit with the fish spear, making sure that the iron hook was stuck into his body. He, thus, killed it. The dugong was brought back to the seashore, pulled by the rope. They cut up the creature and distributed the meat to each and everyone in the community. Everyone got a piece to eat.'

That is the end of the story.

***

After narrating the story given above, Nao was not satisfied with himself as he thought that he could not express well in his native language. He wanted to share with me the details of dugong-hunting at night. Thus, he narrated the following in Andamanese Hindi, which I have translated in English, attempting to keep the original description.

'The dugong is hunted in the sea at night, especially when the moon is still less than half and it is high tide. The reasons are that dugong can be spotted at night because of the fact that wherever it goes, a hue and light goes along with it. Whenever the dugong moves, it leaves behind the spaded water (as the moving ferry does) as well as some sparkles emit from its back. Besides, it emits a kind of torch-like light, *phewe*, in the sea and hence, it can be spotted from a distance. The dugong has an amazing hearing power. One has to be extra quiet while hunting this animal. Even a deep breath by you may trigger its running away. It weighs very heavy.

It is very difficult to hunt dugong because of its sheer weight and size. Not only this, it is capable of running very fast in the water. However, as the dugong swims in the water along with its family and never alone, i.e., male, female, and their young ones, one can also spot the movement when one hears the sound of the young ones looking for their mother. It has been noticed that young ones make similar sounds like those made by chickens. Dugong-hunting is done in a couple of boats or *boya dong*, at least two. However, it is not easy to catch the young ones, because as soon as the mother dugong sees danger, it presses its young one under its side fins and runs very fast in the deep water. Even if it is wounded by harpoon, it runs fast enough to break the rope of the harpoon.

One has to go in the middle of the sea and deep waters and as soon as one spots a dugong; a *roy* 'iron harpoon' is thrown at its back which gets caught so tight that one can then pull the dugong to one's boat by sheer force. Generally, the pulling is done by two people. Once the dugong is near the boat, one or two people jump in the water and tie the dugong around its armpit *um-phong* as well as around its back fins *kobu* which look like an umbrella. Once the dugong is tied in two places it is pulled to the side of the boat. From here on, it is the dugong that pushes the boat towards the coast and hunters stop rowing the boat. They only guide the direction of the boat towards the coast. Once near the shore, they may kill it with a *ballam* (fish spear) in the armpit *um-phong*. Or it may be killed at the shore by a similar method. Whatever way it is killed, it is a very heavy and large animal and it is not possible to either lift it or pull it to the colony. The only way is to roll it down *ecolole* to the village.

Dugong meat is boiled, its thick skin which is generally thicker than 3cm is thrown in the sea. This is because it gets tougher and tougher by days, making it impossible for anyone to do anything with it. Once cut up, it has lots of fat in layers, *elone toleme.* The fat of the dugong looks like ghee and once put in water is soluble *elon-em-shiro.* It is good for children. The intestines are never eaten. The tastiest part of the dugong is the chest, *ara bolilu.* All parts are eaten equally well and one dugong feeds the whole village for a couple of days. The back fin is roasted on fire and hung up in the house. This has a long shelf life, at least for 15 days. Whoever visits the house generally breaks a little amount and chews on it. It perhaps serves as a snack. The dugong's bones are decorated in the house, especially those of backbone and head bone, which are painted in various floral patterns in white clay. The fat of the mammal is used for frying jungle potato. When the bones are boiled, they change their colour to greyish. Dugong can be cooked also the way turtle is cooked on the heated stone.

Another characteristic of the dugong is that this mammal lives like a human family. One dugong may attack another one on its back. One can see the proofs of such fighting in the scars made by the teeth of the attacking dugong. Dugongs are found in plenty near the English Island.'

✳✳✳

Note: The original version with line-by-line translation in English is available in A5 of the Appendix.

Song 10: *ercho taatung tatung, taatung tatung, ercho taatung tatung*
Meaning: Let us go to a cleaner place where we can dance and dance and dance.
Singer: Boa Sr
Tribe: Bo

Scan the QR code
for the audio-visual
recording of this song

Echoes of the Past

Great Andamanese Songs

ELICITING SONGS OF THE VANISHING LANGUAGE

Although songs remain in the memory of the speakers of vanishing languages, the Great Andamanese community in general, has forgotten all their songs. We found very soon that except Boa Sr, the elderly lady in the community, and Nu, another lady in her 50s, no one else remembered any song. Some children were taught to sing prayers in the language and they obliged us.[23]

The Andaman and Nicobar Islands were hit badly by the tsunami on 26 December 2004. Although one official estimate was that we lost more than 5,000 people in the Andaman and Nicobar, yet fortunately, none of the Andamanese tribes had any calamity. The reason was that they were all fishing at the time the tsunami hit the shores and, immediately, knew by seeing the pattern of the sea waves that some havoc was going to approach. Their indigenous knowledge about the unusual kinds of sea waves, such as witnessing the fishes that reside in the twilight zone of the sea and never come to the surface, or the speed of consecutive waves, saved the Onges, the Jarawas, and the Great Andamanese community.

Our plan was to reach Strait Island on that very day, but providence had planned to save us from the disaster, as our papers were not ready to fly from Delhi the week before. We all blessed the inefficiency of the administration, as there was no doubt that if we had made it to Strait Island, either we would have been swept away in the sea or we would have had to stay on a hillock for three days and three nights without any help or supplies. As the entire government machinery was busy rehabilitating the locals, we obtained permission to land on Port Blair only after three months. When we reached Port Blair in March 2005, we realized that members of the community were not happy as they were dislocated from their land and jungle and were made to live in Port Blair in a very crowded guest house called Adi Basera. Although food and water was plenty in the camp, freedom to roam around was very restricted. The environment was not at all conducive to singing and dancing. A baby boy was born in the camp to Licho, a lady who turned out to be very helpful in giving us the language data. We thought we would be fortunate to obtain some birth related songs[24], but alas, no one could oblige us. The general atmosphere was desolate. However, Licho was a good friend and her children keep contact with me about their special events, accidents, sicknesses, and daily routines.

Our regular and frequent visits to the Adi Basera motivated Boa Sr to render some songs in her native language, Bo, one of the 10 north Great Andamanese languages. She was very coperative as can be seen in the audio-visual recordings of her. She managed to translate the songs in her Andmanese Hindi. When we played back the songs to other members of the society for an explanation, all said that they could not

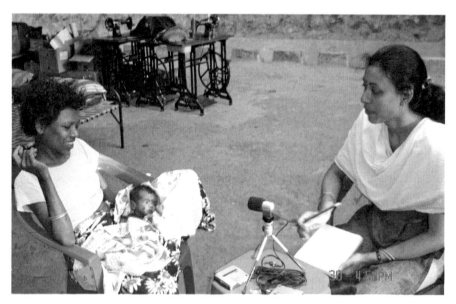

Licho with her new-born in the relief camp after tsunami
(Port Blair, March 2005)

The author, Pao Buddha and Nao Jr at Mayabandar, North Andaman 2008

understand the Bo language very well. Most of the speakers were drawn from the Jeru language. As said earlier in the introductory chapter, the present-day Great Andamanese language is derived from four mutually intelligible northern languages and is a kind of koine. The grammar is based on Jeru, while the lexicon is derived from all four languages, viz. Jeru, Khora, Bo, and Sare. The renderings of Boa Sr thus makes this collection invaluable, as these are the last and the first-ever recordings of the Bo language of the Great Andamanese language family. There are a couple of songs, which even she had forgotten the meaning of, as she informed us that she had not spoken her language for the last 40 years[25]. We could manage to get a couple of lullabies from Boa Sr. It was pathetic that Andamanese children had never heard any lullabies from their parents and, thus, this form of singing was never a part of their upbringing.

After a couple of years of the recordings made in Adi Basera, I was told that there was an elder of more than 80 years of age, from the Karen tribe, living in the north of the Andaman islands, Mayabandar, who learnt the Great Andamanese language as a second language in the early 40s during the British Raj. I was also told that he was much more fluent in the language than anyone else in the community. On hearing this, I convinced Nao to accompany us to Karen village in the northern part of the Great Andaman. We set on our journey, which was more than six hours by road. Once we reached Karen village in Mayabandar it was not very difficult to trace Pao Buddha (this is what he is called by the locals), as his house was known to everyone in the village. After exchanging pleasantries, he came with us to the Public Works Department (PWD) guesthouse, where I had checked in. Knowing that I was interested in documenting the Great Andamanese language, he was filled with joy and started telling me about his friendship with the Chief, Loka, during the 40s, his innumerable hunting escapades in the sea and in the forest. On my request, he rendered a few songs, which are the real treasure trove. His enthusiastic rendering with robust singing of turtle-hunting overwhelmed the historical past. His passion for the Great Andamanese language and the people was obvious, as Nao Jr's eyes lit up and he was overjoyed on hearing these songs. These are given in the accompanying QR code. One could hear him clear and crisp both in audio and video clippings. Since his experience with Loka was more confined to hunting ventures, he sang hunting songs for us. The song he sang was a very rare song of turtle-hunting, as Nao had a very bleak memory of that song, once sung by his grandfather.

I briefly mentioned in Chapter 1 that songs have better staying power than narrations in the life span of a language. We saw the proof in the verbal repertoire of Boa Sr, the 84-year-old woman who turned out to be the single person who could remember some songs. Other community members had not heard Great Andamanese songs in their life and, thus, could not render any. On our insistence, another woman in the 50s, Nu, could remember a couple of songs which have been enlisted in this book. She confessed that she never sang any song to her children. There are no songs related to any ritual. In fact, along with the language, the Great Andamanese culture also has been wiped out. Most young members of the community sing songs from Hindi films and elders opt to remain silent. The music is gone from their lives. The only musical instrument

Recording Boa Sr at Adi Basera (Port Blair December 2005)

Preparing for dance in front of the TV camera 2005

that I saw in Strait Island was a drum called *baumo*, which is played by thumping one foot on it. However, as the community has ceased to sing, it remains neglected on the ground in a corner of a house.

Following is the list of the 25 video songs, their translation in English, and the names of the singers. It will be noticed that all songs are only of one line or a phrase which is sung again and again. The audio-visual recordings of the first 10 songs are available on our website and our YouTube channel (scan the QR codes on the page numbers given in brackets in the table). More such videos will be uploaded to the Niyogi Books website (www.niyogibooksindia.com) from time to time.

Videos Serial No.	Transliteration	Meaning	Singer's Names
01 (pg 53)	*a dure kaiyo laruka, dure kaiyo laruka, dure kaiyo laruka*	This place is not good for living.	Boa Sr
02 (pg 60)	*iyaya khitong kora cheraiyaya, khitong kora cheraiyaya, khitong kora cheraiyaya*	I have been working for so long in the garden and now I am tired and my body is aching.	Boa Sr
03 (pg 67)	*aa jilaptara kamo kamonge ruluchol chalo chalonge ruluchol cholo cholonge rulucho*	Ah! Eyes aiming somewhere and glancing somewhere else! Glancing somewhere else, glancing somewhere else!	Boa Sr
04 (pg 75)	*ngercho tuloe chong chiri chiri ngerchotuloe chong chiri chiri*	A bird with a big beak is searching something here and there.	Boa Sr
05 (pg 81)	*dol koronge tonge jara taikhdunya ila do jara taikhdunya, ila do jara taikh dunya, ila do jara taikhdunya*	The Earth is shaking as the tree falls with a great thud.	Boa Sr

06 (pg 85)	*lele phurjole ṭokhat korme lele*	(Lullaby) I swing your cradle of bamboo back and forth, back and forth.	Boa Sr
07 (pg 92)	*ankile ṭima erachong me ṭorola ai ḍabegri, larola ai ḍabegri, larola ai*	The person who is making a canoe wants blessings so he can make a good canoe.	Boa Sr
08 (pg 97)	*teri dongathebalau kulti* *bangau teri dongathe*	Children are unable to reach up to the fruits on the tree as they are quite high up.	Boa Sr
09 (pg 102)	*dudama kuailang ijokongterbiroe* *dudama kuailarang lodopui jaga terenglo haludapui terenglo haludapui jaga terenglo haludapui jaga terenglo*	Pull it to the shores. Turn over the catch. Turn over the catch quickly! (A turtle-hunting song)	Pa-Aung
10 (pg 108)	*ngercho taatung tatung, taatung tatung, ngercho taatung tatung*	(sung in a group) Let us go to a cleaner place where we can dance and dance.	Boa Sr
11	*chalo batongtha choya chalo*	When older people tell the young boy and girl to work, they don't listen to them.	Boa Sr
12	*o chare dudu pilari ṭana chare dudu pilari*	This song is sung by a group of people, while either going to jungle or going to perform an auspicious task.	Boa Sr
13	*ya kae ya chokbhiṛong khaona khao re chokbhiṛong, khaona khao re chokbhiṛong, khaona khao re chokbhiṛong*	What happened to you? Why are you talking and laughing while eating turtles?	Boa Sr

14	*dara o nuiltaṛa-kalabadal daun meiltaeṛina buthaḍa-kalabadalderina buthaḍa-kalabadal*	The sky is overcast with black clouds, it is going to rain soon.	Boa Sr
15	*je puera thu-thu thua je puera*	Rain-water is flowing down heavily into the canals.	Boa Sr
16	*te marantuke ṭare leiṛote marantuke ṭare leiṛote marantuke*	Cannot sit outside as it is too hot.	Boa Sr
17	*maeme ara kulude komange rera kapagu ralange rera kapagu ralange*	To hunt the dugong we have to row faster and faster.	Boa Sr
18	*ṭokhue rulura thudom tokhue rulura ṭokhue*	Branches of trees hurt your eyes while walking in the jungle.	Boa Sr
19	*nyi polo che pere chiyaya khibana beṭhte iyaya khibanabeṭhte iyaya*	Be careful in the jungle since there are trees which can make your body itch.	Boa Sr
20	*tailukangurphua tailukangurphua chiu*	Song that describes the sound of owl.	Pao Buddha
21	*chokbi ṭema nilela kunyake, nilela kunyake*	They saw a group of baby turtle, baby turtle.	Pao Buddha
22	*rolongo ṭalabar siula rolongo*	The song is sung while digging the earth.	Pao Buddha
23	*phala kailole ilole, phala kailole ilole, phala kailole ilole*	The (strong) waves come and go, come and go.	Pao Buddha
24	*anger chonge tang khoḍo gila gilaa er tang khoḍo gila gila er tang*	There is a bruise on your head.	Boa Sr

We collected some 60 songs, but could decipher only 46, which are given in this chapter. The first line is original, written in Roman. The second line is in the Devanagri script—the script which was given to the language and is currently used by some school-going children. Running translation in English is given in the third line. 38 songs can be heard and 10 of them can be seen through the given QR codes.

In the following pages, the reference of the audio-visual files is given after the name of the singer. The names of the singers, their gender, and age are also given. Not all songs have titles.

SONGS

1. A very popular song of the community

ṭhu mai khach ra re

su ṭhung khora chera

iia iia khe

ṭhung khora chera

ia ia khe

—Sung by Kobo (F 22)

ठु माइ खाच रा रे

सु ठुंङ खोरा चेरा

ईआ ईआ खे

ठुंङ खोरा चेरा

ईआ ईआ खे

Oh father, with this work,

my dried finger-buds burn,

giving me pain and pain,

Baumo, the wooden drum, which is played with right foot while singing

my dried finger-buds burn,

giving me pain and pain!

2. Konjo song of the Jeru language

ṭuṭu li nukhu

thara chaṭo

ṭuṭu li nukhu

thara chaṭo

—Sung by Nao Jr (M 55)

टुटु ली नुखु

थारा चाटो

टुटु ली नुखु

थारा चाटो

Straightening small bamboos,

sweat drops fall.

Straightening small bamboos,

sweat drops fall.

3. A Great Andamanese Prayer

aa bilikhu

kajo bee shorokom

iiḍo shay lule baba kota too

toro chao thut phal be

khile tome robe

ebe aamay aṭoṭa ebii

khaleme bi khaleme

aa reḍa bi khaleme bi khaleme

—Sung by Nu and children; Audio 1

आ बीलीखु

काजो बे शोरोकौम

ईडो शाय लुले बाबा कोता तो

तोरौ चाओ थूत फाल बे

खीले तौमे रौबे

एबे आमाय अटोटा एबी

खलेमे बी खलेमे

आ रेडा बी खलेमे बी खलेमे

O, God, Bilikhu!

We pray to you.

Listen to us.

The storm is nearing,

There is a tide in the sea

Oh father, Oh brothers!

We are helpless!

The boat is running away

Helpless, helpless we are!

4. A Bo Song

ila doo jara tekh dunya

ila doo jara tekh dunya

—Sung by Boa Sr (F 80); Audio 2, Video 4

इला दो जारा तैख दुन्या

इला दो जारा तैख दुन्या

The earth is shaking,

The tree falls with the great roar.

5. A Bo Song

liro temaraṅgtu keṭare

liro temaraṅgtu keṭare

—Sung by Boa Sr (F 80); Audio 4, Video 5

लीरो तेमारानगटू केटारे

लीरो तेमारानगटू केटारे

Cannot sit, it is too hot!

Cannot sit, it is too hot!

6. A Jeru Song

kaptan sablang aka shiṭhiligo o akanga

likha nuṭhungi cheme nacha jao kamlido

be no ṭhongi shoche wena chaja

—Sung by Ilfe (M 27); Audio 5

काप्तान साबलाङ अका शीठीलीगो ओ अकाङा

लिखा नुठुङि छेमे नाछा जाओ कामलीदो

बे नो ठोडि शोचे वेना चाजा

The exact meaning is not available.

Note: This song is about Boa Sr's husband's arrest and imprisonment for six months. Exact meaning could not be deciphered.

7. A Bo Song

thora kaala baadalee

derino botho

thora kaala baadalee

derino botho

—Sung by Boa Sr (F 80); Audio 6, Video 13

थोरा काला बादाले

देरीनो बोठो

थोरा काला बादाले

देरीनो बोठो

Few dark clouds,

pouring all over the place!

Few dark clouds,

pouring all over the place!

8. A Bo Song

er chuuo

taatung tatung taatung tatung

er chuuo taatung tatung taatung tatung

—Sung by Boa Sr (F 80); Audio 7, Video 9

ऐर चूओ

तातुङ ततुङ तातुङ ततुङ

ऐर चूओ

तातुङ ततुङ तातुङ ततुङ

Clean, clean the place,

Dance, dance, dance, dance!

Clean, clean the place,

Dance, dance, dance, dance!

9. A Jeru Song

Ana phalte to rooa bet e-kom

a-jijak roo-o be aomali

alemi

jijak roo ali ali

—Sung by Nu (F 45) Audio 8

आना फाल्ते तो रोआ बेत ए-कोम

आ-जीजाक रो-ओ बे आओमाली

आलेमी

जीजाक रो आली आली

Cutting through the high tide,

Jija's (sister's husband) boat is approaching shaking.

Jija's boat slowly slowly.

10. A Bo Song

er tang khoḍo gila gilaa

er tang khoḍo gila gila

er tang

—Sung by Boa Sr (F 80); Audio 9, Video 7

एर ताङ खोडो गीला गीला
एर ताङ खोडो गीला गीला
एर ताङ
There is a bruise on your head,
a bruise on your head,
on the head!

11. A Bo Song

ṭongo obuliuu

loṭobḍo oeremlaa yera

loṭobḍo oeremlaa

loṭobḍo oeremlaa yera

—Sung by Boa Sr (F 80); Audio 11

टोङो ओबुलिऊ
लोटोब्डो ओएरेम्ला येरा
लोटोब्डो ओएरेम्ला
लोटोब्डो ओएरेम्ला येरा
Crossing the canal by himself,
going all alone to bring food,
going all alone to bring food,
going all alone to bring food.

12. A Bo Song

aanyoo baṛoo nirkono piṛaii

nodo kaagla jaa baa goii

nodo kaagla jaa baa goii

nodo kaagla jaa baa goii

—Sung by Boa Sr (F 80); Audio 14

आज्ञो बाड़ो नीरकौनो पिड़ाई

नोदो काग्ला जा बा गोई

नोदो काग्ला जा बा गोई

नोदो काग्ला जा बा गोई

Go hunt with your bow and arrow,

and bring a pig,

and bring a pig,

and bring a pig!

13. A Bo Song

teri longaṭhe

balao koutli bangoo

teri longaṭhe

balao koutli bangoo

teri long

—Sung by Boa Sr (F 80); Audio 13, Video 18

तेरी लोंगाठे

बालाओ कौउतली बांगो

तेरी लोंगाठे

बालाओ कौउतली बांगो
तेरी लोंग

They are very high up there,
Children are unable to reach up to the fruits!
They are very high up there.
Children are unable to reach up to the fruits!
Very high!

14. A Bo Song

long the phere chiya yaakhi banya beṭheṭe
iia yaakhi banya beṭheṭe iia ya
—Sung by Boa Sr (F 80); Audio 14

लोङ ठै फैरे चिया याखि बाज्ञा बेठेटे
ईआ याखि बाज्ञा बेठेटे ईआ या

The wood in the forest
causes swelling and pain,
swelling and pain!

15. A Bo Song

oo chare dudu pila ri ṭaano
oo chare dudu pila ri ṭaano
—Sung by Boa Sr (F 80); Audio 15, Video 11

ओ चारे दुदु पिला री टानो
ओ चारे दुदु पिला री टानो

Note: The song is sung as a *mantra* to ward away ills. Generally used before hunting escapades or beginning an auspicious action. This is the only song that informed us of the practice of praying. The meaning was not understood by the singer but was convinced of its powers.

16. A Bo Song

Akaee a chok biṛong
khaao na khaao re
chok biṛong
khaao na khaao re
chok biṛong!!
—Sung by Boa Sr (F 80); Audio 16, Video 12

आकाए आ चोक बिड़ोङ
खाओ ना खाओ रे
चोक बिड़ोङ
खाओ ना खाओ रे
चोक बिड़ोङ!!

Eating turtle,
laughing and talking,
move away, move away!
Eating turtle,
laughing and talking,
move away, move away!

17. A Jeru Song

phuṭe birale di birale di
tudik rebe tre
milo re milo

—Sung by Ilfe (M 27); Audio 17

फूटे बिराले दी बिराले दी
तुदीक रेबे त्रे
मीलो रे मीलो

When the sun sets,

find lots of hunt,

find lots of hunt!

Note: The song is code mixed with Hindi.

18. A Bo Song

iiya ya khibanyo beṭhe ṭee
—Sung by Boa Sr (F 80); Audio 18

ईया या खिबाञो बेठे टे

Unable to uproot (it) completely.

19. A Bo song

chalo batho,

ṭha choya

chalo batho,

ṭha choya
—Sung by Boa Sr (F 80); Audio 19, Video 10

चालो बाथो,
ठा चोया

चालो बाथो,
ठा चोया
Many grass hoppers,
My grandmother[26]!
Many grass hoppers,
My grandmother!

20. A Bo Song

menge ara kuluṛe

komangee re

era kaṗa gora langee re

era kaṗa gora langee re

—Sung by Boa Sr (F 80); Audio 20, Video 17

मैडें अरा कुलुड़े
कोमाडें रे
एरा कापा गोरा लाडें रे
एरा कापा गोरा लाडें रे
Spraying water on me,
fast-moving boat.
Swaying in high tide,
swaying in high tide.

21. A Bo Song

Khirme lera coroo kaṭhot

khirme ṭelu rae

byama etyuṭe lorae byamae

ṭyuṭe lorae byamae

ṭyuṭe lorae byamae

—Sung by Boa Sr (F 80); Audio 21

खीरमे लेरा चौरो काठोत

खीरमे टेलू राए

ब्यामा एट्युटे लूराए ब्यामाए

ट्युटे लोराए ब्यामाए

ट्युटे लोराए ब्यामाए

Sweating and sweating,

Burning in the sun. Oh father!

Like turtle-bone is roasted on a fire. Oh Papa!

Papa, like turtle bone roasted on a fire

Papa, like turtle bone roasted on a fire.

22. A Bo Song

A lao lao nata thi thyo khulo

Lao lao nata thi thyo khulo

—Sung by Boa Sr (F 80); Audio 22

लाओ लाओ नाता थी त्यो खूलो

लाओ लाओ नाता थी त्यो खूलो

Strangers of distant land come,

    and remain here.

Strangers of distant land come,

    and remain here.

23. A Sare Song

raa lokra shilo

ṭhi jire alokra shilo ṭhi

—Sung by Boa Sr (F 80); Audio 23

रा लोकरा शीलो

ठी जीरे आलोकरा शीलो ठी

Hit by the hunters,

Pig run helter-skelter on the land.

24. A Jeru Song

ṭha mimiya mukuu karkaa

ana ṭebobi nubi teeka

ṭo maye tomokaṭo pola

—Sung by Nu (F 45); Audio 24

ठा मीमीया मुकू कारका

आना टेबोबी नुबी तेका

टो माये तोमोकाटो पोला

My mother Muku says,

I wish I knew,

to cut out the boat.

25. A Bo Song

aa ṇyya lapra burkhot phala

aa ṇyya lapra burkhot phala

—Sung by Boa Sr (F 80); Audio 25

आ ज्या लाप्रा बुरखोत फाला

आ ज्या लाप्रा बुरखोत फाला

Waves are breaking high up with a thud.

Waves are breaking high up with a thud.

26. A Bo song

ṭokhue rulura thudom ṭokhue

ṭokhue rulura thudom ṭokhue

—Sung by Boa Sr (F 80); Audio 26

टोखुए रूलूरा थूदोम टोखुए

टोखुए रूलूरा थूदोम टोखुए

Branches of the tree hurt your eyes.

Branches of the tree hurt your eyes.

27. A Bo Song

aa jilap tara kamoo kamoonge erulu

cholo chalo chalonge ee rulu

cholo chalo chalonge ee rulu

cholo chalo chalonge ee rulu

cholo chalo chalonge

—Sung by Boa Sr (F 80); Audio 27

आ जिलाप तारा कामो कामोडे ऐरुलु

चौलो चालो चालोडे ऐ रुलु

चौलो चालो चालोडे ऐ रुलु

चौलो चालो चालोडे ऐ रुलु

चौलो चालो चालोङें

Squinted eyes aim somewhere

and look somewhere else.

Squinted eyes look somewhere else

Squinted eyes look somewhere else

Squinted eyes look somewhere else!

28. A Bo Song

aa pebeng ara jee pera thu thu thua

jee pera thu thu thua

jee pera thu thu thua

—Sung by Boa Sr (F 80); Audio 28, Video 14

आ पेबेङ आरा जे पेरा थू थू थूआ

जे पेरा थू थू थूआ

जे पेरा थू थू थूआ

Rain-water flows heavily down the canals,

heavily down the canals,

heavily down the canals!

29. A Jeru Song

anya somra palaka pulia eenro ko eratel

lo bae gir gir lona joldi jara lo

gir gir lona joldi jara lo

—Sung by Tango (F 27); Audio 29 and Ilfe (M27); Audio 36

आज्ञा सोमरा पालाका पूलीआ एनरो को एरातेल

लो बाए गीर गीर लोना जौल्दी जारा लो

गीर गीर लोना जौल्दी जारा लो

Breaking stream and tide pull the boat down,

Slow down the boat fast,

Slow down the boat fast!

30. A Bo Song

erchokh loe chong chiri

erchokh loe chong chiri

—Sung by Boa Sr (F 80); Audio 30, Video 8

ऐरचोख लोए चोङ चीरी

ऐरचोख लोए चोङ चीरी

(His) face has become thin.

(His) face has become thin.

31. A Jeru Song

Similar to the song no.1 this is a shorter version.

khitong kora ceri iaya iiaya

tong kora ceri iaya iiaya

—Sung by Nu (F 45); Audio 31, Video 3 (Sung by Boa Sr)

खिटोङ कोरा चैर ईआया ईआया

खिटोङ कोरा चैर ईआया ईआया

My dried finger-buds burn,

giving me pain and pain!

My dried finger-buds burn,

giving me pain and pain!

32. A Bo Song

ongot bulyaa lii shoroperee noo bulyaa

aajore ree noo bulyala ka

aajoree!

—Sung by Boa Sr (F 80); Audio 32

ओङोत बुल्या ली शोरोपेड़े नो बुल्या

आजोड़े ड़े नो बुल्याला का

आजोड़े!

Worship them who are dead.

Worship your ancestors.

Your ancestors!

33. A Bo Song

aa duure

kaiyoo lorika

aa duure

kaiyoo lorika

duure

—Sung by Boa Sr (F 80); Audio 33

आ दूरे

काइयो लोरीका

आ दूरे

काइयो लोरीका

दूरे

Far are the places,

from the roads!

Far are the places,

from the roads,

faaar!

34. A Jeru Song

(Similar to 1 above but sung by Boa Sr)

yaa yaa

khitong kora cherei

yaa yaa.

yaa yaa

khitong kora cherei

yaa yaa

—Sung by Boa Sr (F 80); Audio 34

या या

खितोंग कोरा चेरेई

या या

या या

खितोंग कोरा चेरेई

या या

Pain and pain,

my dried finger-buds burn,

pain and pain!

Pain and pain,

my dried finger-buds burn,

pain and pain!

35. A Lullaby in Bo

ertaap taap beno

leprong ertaap taap

ertaap taap beno

leprong ertaap taap

—Sung by Boa Sr (F 80); Audio 35

एरताप ताप बेनो

लेपरोंग एरताप ताप

एरताप ताप बेनो

लेपरोंग एरताप ताप

Tap tap sleep,

incense smoke over your head,

tap tap!

Tap tap sleep,

incense smoke over your head,

tap tap!

36. A Jeru Song

le le purjo

le ṭokoṭ koyme

le le purjo

le ṭokoṭ koyme

—Sung by Boa Sr (F 80); Audio 37, video 15

ले ले पूरजो

ले टोकोट कोयमे

ले ले पूरजो

ले टोकोट कोयमे

Swinging up and down,

ants on the tree falling down!

Swinging up and down,

ants on the tree falling down!

Swinging up and down,

Swinging up and down!

37. A Turtle hunting song

dudama kuailarang ijokong terbiroe

dudama kuailarang lodopui jaga tereng lo

haludapui tereng lo

haludapui jaga tereng lo

haludapui jaga tereng lo

—Sung by Pao Buddha (M 80); Audio 38, Video 25.

दूदूमा कूआइलारांग इजोकोंग तेरबिरोए

दूदूमा कूआइलारांग लोदोपुई जागा तेरेंग लो

हालोदापुई जागा तेरेंग लो

हालोदापुई जागा तेरेंग लो

हालोदापुई जागा तेरेंग लो

The exact meaning is not available but it has been included for it rhythmic tenor. The audio and video will apprise the listeners how hunting songs were sung.

38. A Jeru Song

chao thire

lonya eralet phoi

lonya eralet phoi

—Sung by Nao Jr (M 55)

चाओ थीरे

लोन्या एरालेत फोइ

लोन्या एरालेत फोइ

Oh puppy!

Don't bark loud!

Don't bark loud!

39. A Lullaby in Bo

aṭoṭa bonyo

yeo bonyo yeɔ

aṭoṭa bonyo

yeo bonyo yeɔ!

—Sung by Boa Sr (F 80)

अटोटा बोज्ञो

येऔ बोज्ञो येऔ

अटोटा बोज्ञो

येऔ बोज्ञो येऔ!

Sleep son,

sleep! Sleep!

Sleep son,

sleep! Sleep!

40. A Bo Song

no ṭhong icheshe mena
chaja lo likhoobee khule
no shemenatle ṛirono
chaje byatle re
—Sung by Boa Sr (F 80)

नो ठोङ ईचेशे मेना
चाजा लो लीखोबे खूले
नो शेमेनात्ले ड़िरोनो
चाजे ब्यात्ले रे

Note: This song is about Boa Sr's husband's arrest and imprisonment for six months. He was caught by British soldiers for making liquor in Rangat and Mayabandar.

41. A Jeru Song

bi khaleme araiṛa
bi khaleme araiṛa
—Sung by Nu (F 45)

बि खालेमे अराइड़ा
बि खालेमे अराइड़ा
Oh! She has departed
Helpless children!

Helpless children!

Note: This is sung in someone's mourning.

42. A Jeru song

nuli ḍeebee phalte

toma aeruo betekom

aali aali aa maae ruo

aali aali aa maae ruo

—Sung by Konmo (M 13)

नूली डेबे फालते

तोमा एरुऔ बेतैकौम

आली आली आ माए रूऔ

आली आली आ माए रूऔ

Tide has gone away!

On this boat,

the father comes home,

be quiet, be quiet.

By boat comes the father.

By boat comes the father!

43. A Jeru Song

ṭhar bajelaa ra-shukanuu

ṭhar bajelaa ra-shukanuu shukanuu

juroo ulngaa beṭaa bajlata chongkhiu

—Sung by Nao Jr (M 55)

ठार बाजेला रा-शुकानू
ठार बाजेला रा-शुकानू शुकानू
जूरो उलङा बेटा बाजलाता चोङखिऊ

Boat is going berserk in the sea,

berserk in the sea, berserk in the sea,

against the dancing waves recklessly!

44. A Bo Song

ana manes kulii

tarathue phalte

mishu aamaye

krooo be aaom

aali aali mishu aamaye

krooo be aaom aali aali

—Sung by Boa Jr (F 31)

आना मानेस कुली
ताराथूए फालते
मीशू आमाये
क्रोओ बे आओम
आली आली मीशू आमाये
क्रोओ बे आओम आली आली

Go and see,

the tide is low!

My dear father,

comes by boat!

By boat comes my father's body!

Slowly slowly comes by boat.

(the boat is bringing the dead body)

Note: This song was sung on the death of Jirake, the Chief of the Great Andamanese tribe in 2005 when his body was brought to Strait Island from Port Blair by boat.

45. A Bo Song

goo et phulu chika phaka lii joto

jitoo bee goo etkha phaka li jerokon

taraa lot baakayi li jero kontaraa lotbaa

kayi li jero

—Sung by Boa Sr (F 80)

गो एत फूलू चीका फाका ली जोतो

जीतो बे गो एतखा फाका ली जेरोकोन

तारा लोत बाकायी ली जेरो कोन्तारा लोल्बा

कायी ली जेरो

Boats keep coming,

embarking and disembarking.

Men keep working,

swinging with the boats.

46. A Bo Song

aan khile ṭhii maa

era chomer ṭu oroo

laa ee ḍaa gri laa roo

laa ee ḍaa gri laa roo
—Sung by Boa Sr (F 80)

आन खीले ठी मा
एरा चोमेर टू ओरो
ला ए डा ग्री ला रो
ला ए डा ग्री ला रो
Leaves, flowers, bees,
falling on the ground.
Cutting tree for a boat!
Cutting tree for a boat!

Endnotes

1. At present, there are only four semi-speakers with varying degree of competency left in the community. The author is grateful to the speakers, especially Nao Jr and Boa Sr, who, unfortunately, passed away in 2009 and 2010, respectively; Peje and Licho, who died recently on 4 April 2020 for allowing her to experience their world.

2. The project was supported by the Max Planck Institute of Evolutionary Anthropology, Leipzig. I was introduced to the Andaman Islands for the first time during this project. The results of this research are given in my book *Endangered Languages of the Andaman Islands* (2006) (Munich, Germany, Lincom Europa).

3. The project was funded by the Hans Rausing Endangered Language Fund, SOAS, the University of London, 2004 under the ELDP.

4. The narration of Boa Sr is available on the website *www.andamanese.net* that I launched in 2006.

5. Dr Alok Das, Bidisha Som, Arti Kumari, Narayan Choudhury and Abhishek Avatans.

6. No faculty member is permitted to be away from the university within a working semester on a duty leave for more than 28 days. One can stay longer only if one adds vacation days to this leave.

7. Readers are recommended to refer to *Dictionary of the Great Andamanese language. English-Andamanese-Hindi.* (Anvita Abbi, 2012. Delhi, Ratna Sagar.)

8. *A Grammar of the Great Andamanese language. An Ethnolinguistic Study.* 2013. Anvita Abbi, Leiden, Boston, Brill.

9. *Dictionary of the Great Andamanese Language. English-Great Andamanese-Hindi* (with DVD Rom) (2012, Anvita Abbi, Delhi. Ratna Sagar.)

10. *Ethno-ornithology. Birds of Great Andamanese - Names, Classification and Culture,* (2011, co-authored with Satish Pande, Oxford University Press, Oxford, Ela foundation with Bombay Natural History Society).

11. An abridged version of the story was later published by the National Book Trust of India, in English, Hindi, Bangla, Odiya, Tamil, and Telugu, the major Indian languages, and thus, has now reached a large section of children.

12. This was in 2006. The situation has changed since then as the officer-in-charge has retired now.

13. Boa was Nao's estranged wife, who had a child from another man. There is no connection with Boa Sr mentioned earlier.

14. The literal meaning of *pher-ta-jido* in Great Andamanese is 'born out of a bamboo'.

15. *Bolphung* is a place where the Jarawas live. This implies that he ran away to Jarawa jungle, that is, the Baratang area of Middle Andaman. This, perhaps, is the only evidence of possible contact between the Jarawas and the Great Andamanese.

16. Readers may refer to *Ethno-ornithology. Birds of Great Andamanese-Names, Classification and Culture.* 2011 (co-authored with Satish Pande). Oxford University Press, Oxford, Ela foundation with Bombay Natural History Society.

17. Ibid.

18. *Bol* is a large fish and is known to swallow big animals such as pigs etc. It hides its head in the seabed, in the sand and can be recognized by the Andamanese easily as it rests in the muck, in shallow water near the bay area.

19. *Totale* is a nerve inside the belly of the fish.

20. *Jurwachom* are considered heavenly bodies of the water (sea) who protect the Andamanese tribes from any danger.

21. Sea urchin is called *moroi* in Great Andamanese .

22. Though *jurwachom* are known to be the devils of the sea, we have no idea how the devils of the forest are also called by the same name.

23 All the songs given in the QR code, in audio-visual format, were recorded in the post-tsunami relief camp by Dr Alok Das, Research Associate in the project, VOGA.

24 It is very customary to sing specific songs on the birth of a child in Indian culture. It's a group activity symbolizing happiness on a new arrival in the family.

25 Her husband was not from the Bo tribe and thus, she really had not spoken in her variety of the language to anyone for past many years.

26 Mother's mother.

27 *Kaut* is a kind of clay used in making pots.

Appendix

The Original and Line-to-Line English Translation

Due to the 'death' of the language, eliciting a clear, uninterrupted narrative in Great Andamanese was a near-impossible task. Nevertheless, with great difficulty, I managed to cull an original of five stories.

A1. The Great Narrative of Phertajido: A Creation Myth

1. *phertajido o tarphuch tunshongot untoplo jio*
   Phertajido was the first human from Andaman.

2. *phor kotrata thuo*
   He was born out of Bamboo.

3. *urotoy-il eliu phertajido*
   In ancient time, he was named Phertajido.

4. *engkalel engkat phome eremla thitnyo*
   Finding no one around, he lived a solitary life.

5. *kachole me*
   He used to make bows and arrows.

6. *oi ta engkochilel o itachi ek tertok*

   Having made arrows, he tested them by shooting them.

7. *o tungkelo lechik ter toleme*

   He shot arrows all around.

8. *a kambikhir o lechik tertola oika thit bolo inchi*

   Next morning, he went to search for the arrows that he had shot.

9. *o it chongel o inotara chor etchongo*

   Having found one (arrow), he found a water source. He drank the water and thus, discovered drinking water.

10. *bolechik kachil o lechitchong minotara chethul*

    Having made more arrows (he shot more arrows) he found an arrow in the roots of a potato plant.

11. *o iphongil minotcoŋ*

    He found potato in the hollow (of the root).

12. *o tole iebi*

    He took/brought the potato.

13. *du bo o lech inone inche*

    He went to search for the remaining arrows.

14. *o itchongil biutchalo utcong*

    Having found it (arrow) he discovered incense (Hindi: *dhuup*).

15. *o ikhudilo untoplo iebi*

    He returned with a single small piece of incense.

16. *khudi bo olecik tertola eka thit bolo*

    He went to search for more of the shot arrows on the ground.

17. *o it congil kote mele thit cong*

    He found it, *kaut*[27], a very fine soil.

18. *o it chongil u iebi*

    He found it, (Having found it) he brought it over.

19. *u ik khuni*

    He (took some of it and) returned.

20. *koṭek phechi bano*

    (He) made a pot/vessel out of the soil.

21. *o i taphai*

    He dried it.

22. *irem lamil phech ta ṭol eraṭeshe*

    Having hardened the pot, he cooked the potato in the pot.

23. *phechta ṭolera ishe iboi u ïji*

    He put the pot with the potato on the fire, boiled/cooked it and ate it.

24. *u ïjite utborṭhul*

    While eating, he thought.

25. *otum arphuch teka u ebukhu ebano*

    He made a dummy in the shape of an Andamanese woman.

26. *u ṭhichal arachaka o ara aṭe kubi*

    He put it (the dummy) on the platform and lighted a fire.

27. *a taphai t nol*

    He dried it well.

28. *bo kokacholil u tum bot khachol o eule*

    While giving the final touches (to arrows) he turned back to see.

29. *ṭhicha tuttaraal kot tun tabino be*

    Kaut lay asleep on the platform.

30. *bo araaṭ eku bi unchi*

    He went again to kindle the fire.

31. *bo o koka col*

    And he resumed peeling the bow.

32. *bo o tum botkhachol ṭhicha eule*

    He turned back again to see the platform.

33. *amimi akoṭ atashuny kelonyil engkhile*

    The body of the mother, Kaut, turned sideways and shook.

34. *phertajiḍo u tum borcho*

    Phertajido was happy with himself/was satisfied.

35. *aranṭoyal u araaṭikubi unchi*

    Then he stood up and went to kindle the fire.

36. *kokacholik malail u shiḍik utchonne*

    Having got tired by making the arrows, he went to hunt.

37. *o rakrel u ikhunni ṇyo ak*

    Having found the game, he came back home.

38. *akang tutolel ṭhicha kak*

    He glanced at the platform.

39. *ṭhicha terlokho*

    There was nothing on the platform; the platform was empty.

40. *utung bo kalui-il*

    He was heart-broken; he became melancholy.

41. *o ra talel chyak khidi koṭ belo*

    'He put down the (hunted) pig, "Where did Kaut go/get lost?"'

42. *o tung bo chaayik akauno*

    With a heavy heart, he sat down.

43. *amimi akot nyokotrata o a phertajidot kholet lameme*

    Mother Kaut tired herself laughing at Phertajido from inside the house.

44. *phertajido erachil atum bot khachl eule*

    Surprised, Phertajido turned back to see (where the laughter was coming from).

45. *akote eule*

    He saw Kaut.

46. *phertajido ematil unchi*

    Phertajido went to her running.

47. *akotek terchoichil kot-ek ngolome*

    Embracing the *kaut*, he burst out crying.

48. *danto nenchuo thit nyome*

    Then they lived in their own place.

49. *nutun thireemil nutunthirechophe*

    Their children had children and they were many.

50. *u ne boimil*

    They married each other.

51. *u thiret thire chophemil*

    Children gave birth to many more children. Children's children were many.

52. *phertajido emboi akote ikjiral*

    Phertajido asked his wife, Kaut.

53. *pharoko* *bikete*

    Make rope.

---

* *Pharako* is a kind of rope, which is made out of a creeper by the same name, 'pharako'. The rope is especially known for its strength.

54. *um pharako inchil pharakok uni*

   He came back with *pharako* twigs for her.

55. *emboi akoṭ ekjiral pharakobi bole*

   He said to his wife Kaut, 'Make a rope out of it.'

56. *eralobum o itaungkochil etchalo*

   She made such a long rope that it coiled into a heap.

57. *pharako tujuphul phertajiḍo meobi kochobil*

   Phertajido tied a stone at the end of the rope.

58. *o erkeṭol o ekterṭoe ṭaut umikhuk*

   He swirled it and then hurled it (the stone) at the sky in the middle.

59. *chyal erensholokil o ekṭeno atachi*

   He pulled it (the rope) down to check where it (the rope) was stuck.

60. *u erṭeterel*

   It (the rope) was stuck.

61. *kenmo erkeṭil*

   (He) twisted the threads of the rope.

62. *kenmo choṭome*

   It (the thread) became very taut and curled.

63. *kochop*

   He tied it (the rope).

64. *emboi koṭe ekjiranchil*

   He went to tell his wife, Kaut.

65. *ṭhu shongak motkocho kak ṭhut chonebom*

   'I will go up above, there in the heaven.'

66. *thu thibi ole*

    'I will see the place.'

67. *shitane thi bi*

    'How is that place?'

68. *motkocho kak thambikhir thut chonekom*

    'Up and above us, I will go (to heaven) tomorrow (next morning).'

69. *akambikhir utchone*

    Next day, he went away.

70. *o rephul motkochokak thi ole mil*

    Having climbed up, he saw/discovered the place and returned.

71. *o tarphuchine chophe tchong*

    He found many people like himself.

72. *aka mele thiloel u uni*

    Having seen the place he came back.

73. *emboi akote jira lolkoch mutaraphuch kenyo*

    He told his wife, Kaut, 'People like us live up there.'

74. *thi nole mebe*

    That place is very good.

75. *emboi kote kjiral khate thengotchone*

    He told his wife, Kaut, 'Let us go there.'

76. *akote akatekhuk phil*

    Kaut did not like his proposal.

77. *shitane thengotun thirene thibitmo*

    'How shall we leave the place of our children?'

78. *bo aphertajido ikjira*

    Then Phertajido said,

79. *thengotunthireni arbitta kamo theng otchone*

    'If we convince our children, we can go.'

80. *nutun thiren aranyil u ni aretta*

    Having gathered his children, he addressed them.

81. *phertajido ikjiram thu thire khoittak^he neli thibika lileke*

    Phertajido says, 'My children, have patience! You all keep silence. Let there be peace on this land.'

82. *ngale mimi ngale may thiyo mungili arbittakom*

    'We, your mother and father, both of us want to speak to you, make you understand.'

83. *khilele mungili thibit nyo pho*

    'We will not stay over here with you all.'

84. *motkochua menyo be*

    'We will go up above us (heaven).'

85. *khilele ngole thibit nyotnole*

    'You all live here happily.'

86. *dikho muntara liu bo*

    'That's enough, we have completed our time here, our time here is over.'

87. *itto tekhamo mutchonebom*

    'Right now, we are going/leaving.'

88. *nu rephul pharako ikku beling*

    Having climbed up (the rope), they cut off the rope.

A2. The Tale of Maya Lephai

1. *Maya Lephai ara lephai embui jul. uek thikion wenthikiol wek emboya.*
   a khimil tale neiciral ne boi nol phobe eboinol phobe oashyu ik thibik
   nioma ona bingu phulu

   Lephai was a young man, who loved a girl immensely. He wanted to marry her, though his friends warned him that the girl was seen with another man and did not bear a good reputation. He did not believe his friends and said,

2. *sho sho thu ekthemboya. choe choe shitan boik nembui. mu tiri chokhibi,*
   katangertubui thatanertubui

   'No, no, I am going to marry her,' and he did marry her eventually. They had four children thereafter, two boys and two girls.

3. *boa kam bi khere unun shidik chil. uthi mike kara lili kara lili. uthimike*
   kala lili ibui ot tebol. tua thire nu thibi morol.

   One fine day, he went to hunt in the jungle to catch some game for his children. Somehow, he got delayed in coming home. When he came back, he found his wife missing. When he looked inside the house, he found his children crying and there was no sign of their mother. He asked them,

4. *ono boil , molit chae khudi molo bon*

   'Why are you crying?'

5. *toboya*

   The children replied,

6. *thamay, thamimi te bolbo*

   'Father, our mother has run away.'

7. *chiak ngale mimi bolbo*

   'Where did the mother go?'

8. *ko*

   'We don't know.'

9. *tunguli ṭiebe ngolot ṭhoa kaṭhiet bolom. unijiral ngatuing borchol, ngatuing borchol ngamaik iami Nok ṭhik ngomi.*

   Hearing this, Lephai said, 'Try to be quiet and have patience. I am sure she must have gone to her parents. I will go and look for her'.

10. *wek te bol. waka ṭhit bolol. wet chong bolol. bo unil uta kath rio noko bo-il amami mibu?*

    Lephai looked for his wife everywhere, but could not trace her. When he returned home empty-handed, his children confronted him, 'Abba, did you find our mother?'

11. *ṭhot chong phuto*

    'No, I did not find her.'

12. *bou batil binal*

    He (Lephai) slept that night with a heavy heart, as he was very sad and worried.

13. *boa ka mikhila kaṭhit bolon chilo na moboe mil. tara chulu ara julu ka bingu nana julu ka bingu. nara julu ka bingo. chyalnio. boing ṭainga. boing ṭaingar nir nurola.*

    Next day, he woke up and went again into the forest to look for his wife. He enquired from many people if they had seen her whereabouts. Someone told Lephai that a fire was seen at night on top of the hill. 'What is the name of that place?' Lephai enquired.

    'Bontaing,' People told him.

14. *koel thona thi chikom batil*

    He thought of visiting the place at night.

15. *may dikhongoma mit changmo?*

    'Did you find the mother?'

16. *otong thire konot otoe*

    'No, children, I could not find her.'

17. *thire ner niu mil nubolik. oitaot lel onemato lelong. mayalephae robitutaot lel. roadilu. okothula maya lephae maya no necho, one ma neoleme. nubolikhil, nubolikhil one mato naraletong.*

    As soon as the children went off to sleep, he left the house very quietly and stealthily. He went to the seaside and lowered the boat in the water. He started rowing the boat towards the place where the locals had seen the fire. When he came near Bontaing, he saw the light of the burning fire. He waited till the fire got extinguished. 'It seems they have gone to sleep now,' he mumbled.

18. *nara letong. ot niol nara letong. ve matoet phiret jol.*

    He stealthily approached the house and saw Noe sleeping with his wife. He was so outraged that initially he thought of killing him outright in his sleep.

19. *kiurtumbot delotairbingul. hade thuer khiretal thu ephire.*

    'No, first, I will wake him up, and then I will kill him so that he knows who has killed him and why,' he thought.

20. *erkhilul. erkhilul okongel elerchulukhilueolel mayalephae maya nokongil oyolil lephaeertoya oephiri oerkhit phiri. lektaephiril ertongekom teterel. erteterel botebolot joloaka kabhit ekachorok phichil lej. ubutho.*

    Lephai then woke Nu up. As soon Noe opened his eyes, he looked up and saw Lephai standing over him. Before he could rise, Lephai shot an arrow in his shoulder joint, so that his arm got stuck to the side as if it was stitched to his side. Immediately, he shot another arrow and hit his kneecap completely jamming his movement. Noe fell downright there.

21. *ubuthol ite iboikoi utun te khul utebol. maya lephae otbota ephiri. ngalto ule chil puto toe chatophul boaka melil omayano unchil. ot bot ulu ot bot phire lechik butho*

In the meanwhile, Lephai's wife woke up and, seeing the whole scene, started running away. Lephai shot her immediately in the back, right where the arrow could pierce her heart. His wife fell on the ground and died immediately.

22. *boa maya lephae et mo may anonchil.*

Maya Lephai then went back to Noe and said,

23. *wek puya wek embuya oketa ekto boya. Maya nonchil wek jiral chae kude uthe boek te bolbo.*

'Why did you run away with my wife?' He asked Noe.

24. *ma cha shyut phoebo*

'Could you not find any other woman in the world other than my wife?

25. *tae ta itomodan tuthe chibo.*

'That is why I want to kill you.'

26. *thut them boekho tuthun thiro korata thitan tune thit chiko.*

'Little do you know with what difficulties I have raised my children.'

27. *them boi kiteka tunguthe jire belejira be teka. tho ek themboik phulo*

'If you were in love with my wife, you should have told me earlier. Had you told me earlier, I would never have married this girl.'

28. *ae koding otha tangeng phir khudi. tha tanga ra lilere. chae kolik.*

On hearing all this, Noe requested Lephai, 'Why don't you kill me right away? Kill me. Why are you giving me this pain?

29. *sho shothong ata theng philubi othatha*

'No, no, I will not kill you right away.'

30. *thungata ade*

'Wait, I will not kill you now.'

31. *tokontobolo bataithi thung ata thara jibu. tataekhobi raliemo. thunga ta kemphilbo*

'Till I am finished talking to you and till I have emptied my heart, I will not kill you. I will force you to suffer for some time.'

32. *nikho tha tekho biraje*

(Lephai) kept telling him his woes and when he had expressed his anger to his heart's satisfaction, he said,

33. *ekho thot boberaliu. akakang kerta cheo lotil oek boerdile nu ukha thu*

'I have said it all. Now, I will kill you', and he drew a knife from his chest-guard and pierced it through the heart of Noe.

34. *ne lolil tembo mayanu. boelolil ngot chalol ongora cherebil ne lolil tembo mayanu. ongeshui.*

Lephai then picked up his wife's body and laid her next to the dead Nu's body. He broke down the thatch, cut up all the wooden walls, and collected all the artifacts of the house and piled up everything on the two bodies. Lephai then set the house on fire.

35. *ongeshui.*

He, thus, burnt both the bodies (his wife's and her lover's).

36. *bolphung bolphung-at nge-tebol not ong-cham*

Went away to Bolphung. (Thereafter, he returned home. He was very sad and quiet. He hadsome plans but dare not discuss with anyone.) He picked up his children and went into the deep forest of Bolphung. No one has ever seen Maya Lephai or his children since then.

Note: Nao varies between the name 'Noe' and 'Nu'. Both refer to the same person. The name Bolphung refers to a water cave near the current Jarawa reserve.

A3. Maya Jiro Mithe

Following is the exact transcription of the story of Maya Jiro Mithe in the Great Andamanese language. As expected, there are several disconnected dialogues, as Nao was not very fluent in the narrative mode of the language. Nao translated every Great Andamanese sentence in Andamanese Hindi with explanation. He alternates between the names 'Bol' and 'Bom' of the fish that occupies the centre stage in the narrative. Both refer to large fish which can swallow big animals whole.

1. *a jiro miṭhe shidina*
   Jiro Mithe went hunting.
2. *u shiḍil ontae phulo*
   He didn't find any prey.
3. *o khatak chong ilu eraphur luṭit burliutara chorel akaono*
   He found a muscle-like fish by the name Kata and sat down to clean it.
4. *toira phulrlu bingoi khuriṭ okhimin ena echae trek*
   The more he cleaned the fish, the bigger it became.
5. *bol aingaet wet oet o khinaril otchalo*
   Whatever the dispensable element came out, he collected.
6. *boa kancha ral boik ora phuli bin chil bolbeiji tan to yeṭemel ephu*
   While he was sitting in a squatting position (by the seashore, with his back to the sea), a large Bol fish came from behind and swallowed him whole in the sitting position.
7. *ejilia raphetekotle*
   Took him to the deep sea.

8. *ara lilel roa kat hit bolo*

   It had been two-three days since he had gone; there was no information of him.

9. *tono a raṭhit cong*

   They found the place where he had cleaned the Kata.

10. *noit ner lilimil*

    They began wondering, what would have happened to him (Mithe).

11. *chya kajiro miṭhet chok meraṭhit chongo*

    Someone among them said, 'He must have gone somewhere on the land.'

12. *boljlekya ko khijre khiko balont*

    Then someone said 'If he had to go somewhere, he would have taken his bows and arrows'.

13. *ot chonam otokoe bimb*

    'He would not have left his bows and arrows.'

14. *o ete sil puo erapur lebinchi*

    'He would have eaten it, after cleaning.'

15. *yejilie ṭemiloji*

    'He would have eaten it all.'

16. *toakaunut jilu yetemili*

    'He must have gone into the stomach of Bol in sitting/squatting position.'

17. *ye kortle*

    Having eaten Bol.

18. *at oboliekhu*

    'Bol must have eaten him up.'

19. *ir khurur*

    'Maybe.'

20. *ek ner nitenoir kaṭhietbolo*

    Wherever the Bol went, the water became dirty.

21. *phiter biri utchonge kaka shoro*

    Following the trail of the dirty water, they went deep into the sea.

22. *shiro kakek otleko*

    They searched for him in the deep sea.

23. *phaṭkan tabaebei ṭoro kaṭhit bolng otchong*

    Phatka was knowledgeable (about sea life) and thus, he found the fish.

24. *u eishoro loṭtoraotli*

    He tried hitting the Bol with a bamboo but couldn't reach it.

25. *phaṭkaṭ toraotli*

    Phatka and others also tried.

26. *ngo ttoṛa otlime*

    They couldn't succeed.

27. *chit anmetchin*

    'How will we do it?'

28. *chit anme tut kolonte libie*

    'We cannot do this, call Kolo.'

29. *kolo ṭulubung kolo ṭulubung*

    'Kolo, where are you?' (He hears them).

    In the narration in Hindi, Nao explains that on hearing his name, Kolo rushes to the spot thinking his friends must have found Jire.

30. *chia ijiyo ?*

    'Where is he?'

31. *khilil khilil khidi …biriu*

He observes that if we hit the fish belly it will injure the person inside.

32. *irchoka ṭhit bolo*

Bol's head was buried in the sand

33. *e uleṭ nolae chia kercho*

'See which side is its (Bol's) head,' (Kaulo said).

34. *ot chok oṭkoṭra li*

'Hit him on the head.' After this, Kolo instructed:

35. *deko thu it orob er-choboe*

'Tie all the boats; otherwise, we will be scattered.'

36. *kwara buliṭ hitchobil nata ochor cho ṭhingo*

Having hit the fish on the head, Kolo pulled all the boats in one line by a rope.

37. *inet ṭhut ḍilo ṭhimikhu bokresh*

Wherever he went through the jungle it created a ditch or when it went around any land piece, it created an islet.

38. *ṭibokreshemul thiriṭhunṭhilo banome*

It created several islets

39. *kolo ataemphil*

(Finally,) Kolo killed the fish

40. *roa bir cobe mae*

'Tie the fish to the boat.'

41. *o ituḍelo buliu ṭhi bo kraesho*

Many islets were created by the impact.

42. *ṭhi bokraesho tuḍ ḍila kata*

Islets were created.

43. *emalae*

Got tired.

44. *malae noishoro noit an emphil*

They were tired after killing the Bol.

45. *noya kotra torin*

They tore open the stomach (of Bol).

46. *bole kotra torin noye lotil noye banesheri*

They took him (Jiro Mithe) out from its stomach and saw that his limbs had become stiff by sitting in a squatting position.

47. *o benil jiro miṭhe benil*

Being inside, Jiro Mithe had become very soft.

48. *noara chal noaraṭ ikubi*

They built a platform and lit the fire under it. One of them asked, 'How to eat that huge fish?'

49. *ara cha prollae me bolbe phute kuana*

'We will cut up the Bol.'

50. *mephute meji*

'We will eat the cut-up pieces.'

51. *nin se meku kube linge milnui buli*

Took their respective pieces and went.

52. *mai dit dithi boel kubelingi*

The children of Kolo shouted, 'Father give us the cut-up pieces, we will burn them.'

53. *ṭhui se*

'We will roast them.'

54. *ṭhibi lobong*

(He) gave them a long piece.

55. *chi ṭhung likube lingu*

(He) cut it and gave it to them.

56. *thire ishuil*

The children cooked it on fire.

57. *keba ḍie chatho id luṭ perṭo bolo*

    Kolo turned around and saw that the children had put the
    Bol on fire.

58. *I shuel iphiluṭ peṭ*

    By putting it on fire, the stomach (of the fish) swelled up.

59. *kolobe kautleome*

    Kolo did not know that.

60. *taṭale philutpeṭhelithit ṭhe*

    Totale (nerve of the fish) was not to be cut.

61. *itthebil nesuntaji tutbech*

    Everyone had become birds.

62. *itthebil nesuntaji tutbech i-baṭchi*

    Everyone became birds of their individual names.

63. *a choiṛ atphoi*

    Turned back to see.

64. *tum boto leim achio ṛat phoi*

    Turned back to see, but could not find anything.

Then he looked for Jiro Mithe, whether he was dry or not, but even he
was not there. He as well as Kolo had become birds.

A4. The Water God Maya-Kobo and Jire

This is how Nao Jr narrated the story in the Great Andamanese language.

1. *ṭho a maya kobo a jire nerta*
   Now I tell you the story of Maya-Kobo and Jire.

2. *a Jire larabi kauṭ chaungde leshare*
   Once Jire went hunting with his friends for turtles at night.

3. *Maya-kobo ong-yoluubenui. phauruket chokbi*
   Maya-Kobo was sleeping on an ancient turtle in the sea.

4. *a Jire chokbi bikremil ikre. tara shulo vuithudil. phauroket chokbi thudil.*
   That night, Jire hunted many turtles. He hunted many. He killed the big turtle.

5. *vetbol a Maya kobot chu ut ṭhut. o yolilo chokbi elilthudi. erentaa liek shungi thuth*
   The arrow hit the head of Maya-Kobo. He did not know that Maya-Kobo was sleeping on it. He was killed by an accident. It went through and through his forehead.

6. *o ithuuthi ro kak rephul. toro kakre phul a ki ther le lame bo me taoi. itakhi itare phaye etallelabo*
   'Row the boat as I am giddy. I am nauseating.'

7. *ṭhibie erle lame. ngoik krokoteshil. birdi*
   As soon as he reached the shore he vomited and collapsed.

8. *Maya-kobo o chokbit baul oṭ chot thudil*
   Maya-Kobo's head was hit, while he was on the back of the turtle.

9. *nyola kobo maya-kobo konyel 'aa Jire erchubit kuthulo. chokbi tokbol. nyara eren thi chaya.'*

He reached home and told his wife that his head was wounded while he was on the back of the big turtle. 'Jire hit me when I was on the back of the turtle. You bury me in the earth.'

10. *aka Maya a kama mime jirabi. nejiral nauya kroya olel.*

'Tell his father and mother that Jire's boat must be approaching the shore.'

11. *aakamimi notum bochai. roa ul akum tesik nothi molo. autauraulel.*

His parents were sad. As soon as the boat reached the shores, parents started crying.

12. *ullel erlila lu bu tul emphil*

As he reached the shores he collapsed and died.

13. *emphililo Maya-kobo unne jiral mille thai ke billiemo temphil bemo otchobi ollae thercho tauebe ollae. ther cho taue be phonggaye mole ole. cher co ter tich titabi. to noa ka tekhonerbido.*

Maya-Kobo tried to convince his wife that after he was buried in the earth, she should dig up his grave after a few days to confirm that he was indeed shot in the brain. 'You dig up my skull and check…a hole in the skull.' People started believing him.

14. *emphilil both koel jngoel johongge noe cho opongil. maya-kobo cho opongil. o ithut ke sath okonel.*

After his death, people dug up the earth and found a hole in his head. Blood like substance was there.

A5. When We Hunted Dugong

The following narration is a glaring sample of a vanishing language. The narrator had lost the art of narration as it can be seen in short phrases, unconnected events, and disturbance in linearity, for which the later event is reported earlier and the earlier event is reported later. After narrating the following piece, the narrator again described in detail how dugong hunting was done.

1. *thamaya maro tamimik uthe uthon thire khukh anu*
   My father, Moroi, took me and my mother.

2. *yangbui ka loka*
   My mother's name is Loka.

3. *ume lara kakh*
   He took us for hunting.

4. *umelara kakh at chongil muntaepho*
   He did not find any game.

5. *bo u ro ta terbui nomacho kak laral koch mamboro*
   There was another boat side-by-side, for hunting in the sea, with us.

6. *umelara lokotae pholo koronyolil pheuwentol*
   Suddenly, we saw a dugong. There was light emitting.

7. *u i thudil*
   We hit him.

8. *ervora ko talme*
   He went around our boat.

9. *e meo rakotel eror kotel jul emebok thut*

    He took a round of our boat from the back. My father didn't understand why he was running in the opposite direction.

10. *bok thut*

    He hit our boat in the centre.

11. *bok thut thudil mer wobe kon tolo*

    From beneath the boat, he hit it in the centre.

12. *thir binu thamimi ther robirajo*

    I was sleeping at the back of the boat and my mother was rowing the boat.

13. *rotercho tam thamai thut ilerok tebol imbok thulel akathi telenglol thituyet tengil naolit phul*

    The dugong hit the boat so hard that it broke. My father shouted for help, but in the dark, nothing was visible as what exactly happened.

14. *ota amimilyu mambororowo kakilun telil*

    Mother called for the other boat that was with us.

15. *bolera cobli ektebol to mambolkakh wobi khamoin te thamimin telil nomatel*

    Hearing the voice, the other boat came near us and my mother and I mounted on the other boat.

16. *bonoma maikat thamai katit bolo tha*

    Seated in the other boat, we set out, looking for my father.

17. *tanwa kathit eleltho tara mikhu tele*

    We shouted for him.

18. *tara mikhu*

    In the distance in the middle of the sea (we saw him).

19. *tul me choa kroak chilno koron tara bullik rola kambal katirbi rolo*

    He opened the rope, got in the boat and then jumped into the water to tie the rope around the dugong.

20. *noitaul noishoro*

    They pulled the rope near the boat and hit the (the dugong) with a fish spear.

21. *noim phong shorol noitan imphil*

    They killed him in the armpit.

22. *noikrok kunyil nyol noik kutil chayak nyut khi buti*

    They distributed the dugong meat to everyone. All went home with a piece of dugong.

23. *i koira li*

    That's the end of the story.

Afterword

By the beginning of the 21st century, the Present-day Great Andamanese (PGA) language, the sole survivor from the Great Andamanese language family, was staring extinction in the face, as the last few 'rememberers' of PGA had reached the final stage of forgetting their heritage language. So, a group of languages that had been spoken in the Andamans for millennia, since prior to the establishment of British control in the 1860s, was about to disappear, almost without trace. Fortunately, one intrepid Indian linguist, Professor Anvita Abbi, decided that this should not be allowed to happen, that the linguistic and cultural knowledge of the last speakers of PGA should be recorded and analyzed for posterity, not only for the benefit of scientists (linguists, anthropologists, and others), but also for the future generations of the community to have access to this important part of their intangible heritage.

The salvation work undertaken by Professor Abbi was far from easy, considering the practical problems of conducting linguistic fieldwork and compiling an audio-visual documentation in an environment with minimal infrastructure—only two hours of electricity daily—with the additional initial reluctance of the community members to open up their world to outsiders, who only too often are identified with the forces that have led to the loss of their culture and of their self-esteem. It is fortunate that a scholar with Professor Abbi's tenacity, as well as her scientific credentials, was available and willing to conduct this work. She has rendered the documentation of the language by recording stories and songs, and has also compiled a substantial grammar and dictionary of the language, the first truly modern linguistic studies of any of the indigenous languages of the Andaman Islands. This is truly ground-breaking work that has saved a language from oblivion.

My colleague, Raoul Zamponi, and I are working to complement Professor Abbi's work by providing an up-to-date linguistic analysis of the available documentation of the Great Andamanese languages from the 19th and early 20th centuries, with the focus on the languages from the south of the archipelago, while Professor Abbi has worked with North Andamanese varieties. The first major fruit of our labour is the title, *Grammar of Akabea*, which has been published this year. Throughout our work, we have been conscious of the extent to which we are walking in Professor Abbi's footsteps, albeit with the advantage of comfortable locations in Italy and California, where we did not have to be on the continuous lookout for crocodiles and sea snakes!

I write these words as the COVID-19 pandemic rages without any clear signs of abatement, and only a few days after learning that the pandemic has now reached the indigenous inhabitants of the Andaman Islands. The last few centuries have seen continuous assaults on the integrity and the existence of indigenous cultures across the world, not necessarily through ill-will, but often, as the anthropologist Alfred Radcliffe-Brown said of the effect of British rule on the indigenous peoples of the Andamans, through 'carelessness and callousness'. He was referring to the decimation of the Andamanese populations through introduced diseases in the late 19th century. Every time we say that next time we will do better. Professor Abbi has shown us the way to make our good intentions a reality. I encourage linguists in India and across the world to follow her example, to document endangered languages and cultures not only to benefit science, but also to raise the self-esteem of indigenous peoples by revealing their contribution to the cultural heritage of humanity itself.

The current volume constitutes the author's research on the history and culture of the Great Andamanese and her adventures in working with them; 10 stories in English translation (with the original text of five of them in the Appendix); and 46 songs in the original (in both Latin and Devanagari scripts) with their English translations. Links to her recordings have also been provided. The volume is a great initiation for readers to the wonderful world that Professor Abbi has opened up for us.

Bernard Comrie
Santa Barbara, California, September 2020

Acknowledgements

This little book would not have been possible without the help, cooperation, and love of many friends, colleagues, and the community of the Great Andamanese, especially the elders. I am indeed in debt of Nao Jr, Boa Sr, Licho, and Nu, who rendered the Andamanese stories and songs.

The biggest help came from the School of African and Oriental Studies (SOAS), London, who facilitated the work under the project *Vanishing Voices of the Great Andamanese* (VOGA, *www.andamanese.net*), which not only built the foundation of the research, but also nurtured the research to see its culmination in all realms of language documentation—grammar, dictionary, indigenous knowledge, oral tradition, and secrets of sustainable ecology, zoological encyclopedia, and world-view.

I am thankful to my team members of the VOGA project, Dr Alok Das, Dr Narayan Chaudhuri, Abhishek Avatans, and Palyan, the social worker, who accompanied me to Strait Island. I am very grateful to Alok for his perseverance in obtaining songs from Boa Sr as can be witnessed from the video recordings. In a society which had stopped singing indigenous songs, he encouraged the young and the old to sing for us and they did oblige us with a feeling of gratefulness, as they marvelled at themselves that they remembered many of the songs. Least did they know that songs reside latently in the memory house, till someone makes them open its door. Narayan's dedication to elicit the first creation myth of the Great Andamanese language is a story worth telling in every linguistic fieldwork class. His patience, generosity, and cool behaviour helped Nao in memorizing the forgotten tales.

I am thankful to the Director, Grassi Museum Leipzig and the Curator, Carola Crebs, who made it possible for me to see, touch, and feel the 19th-century artefacts of the Andaman. Some of the pictures in this book are from that museum.

I am grateful to Meenakshi Bharat for putting this book together, for going through the first draft of the manuscript, and giving some wonderful suggestions. I am fortunate to have constructive suggestions of Sukrita Paul Kumar, who always had very appreciative ears in listening to the Great Andamanese stories and for encouraging me to collate them in a volume. Without her I would have not been introduced to Niyogi Books.

A special thanks to Satish, who helped me translate the songs and forever encouraging me to document this magnificent language in all its realms.

Time is ticking fast, as the language is going into oblivion. No one is left in the community who can narrate any story or sing more than two songs in the language. In this dismal atmosphere, I am thankful and happy that Niyogi Books has decided to bring out this book which is not less than an accumulated edifice of an oral tradition which was not heard, neither seen, nor felt by the world before this.